BOOK 1

The pain was real. The ache of long-ago broken bones and the cold spot in my chest. It was there. An icy hunk of steel. Sometimes it chilled like a winter breeze. Sometimes it froze like an icy dagger through my heart. Always, it was there to remind me of what I'd lost and what I'd done. But I didn't want to remember. Didn't want to face the truth. So there was the pain.

I thought it was my problem. The steady chill. The sudden spikes. Little did I know. It was the solution. I had other problems. Booze and bills and pills for the moment. Things would get worse. A lot worse. Just then, at the beginning of my story, I was caught up in the web of addiction. As I recall, it was fall, and I sat in my office on Berry Boulevard. Looked through the grimy window. Watched the dirty cars go by. Crushed the round pills into white powder.

Five. Maybe six. Whatever. I snorted the crushed Oxi, and heat rushed through my body. My arms and hands and face flushed with heat, and I felt like a sugar cube in a cup of hot tea. Melting. Melting. Dissolving in the warm liquid bliss. My body faded, but the pain persisted. For just a moment, it remained. A cold blue star deep inside. It held on until it was the last part of me. All that was left after the Oxi rush. But that also faded to the warmth.

All tension gave way to it, and I slumped on my wooden office chair. My hands hung from the ends of the armrest, and my

4

JIMMIE STAR, BODHISATTVA

Volume 1

By
Alex B. Stephens

Anima Press

Louisville, Kentucky

JIMMIE STAR, BODHISATTVA

Volume 1

head tipped forward. My cheeks hung loosely, and my breathing settled to a slow surge. All was darkness and warmth and the slow whumping of my sluggish heart.

**

The bell on the door dinged, and I struggled to wake. Blinking and rubbing my eyes, I looked up to see the silhouette of a small woman standing across the desk from me. Slowly, my eyes focused on her dark form, then the details of her face came gradually into resolution. Plump lips. Slightly knitted brows. Almond-shaped, yellowish brown eyes. I looked into them and drifted back toward unconsciousness.

"Thank goodness for G.P.S."

I rubbed my eyes.

"Didn't know this part of town existed."

"Utility poles and cell towers." The words came out garbled. I tried to straighten up in my chair but couldn't support the weight of my head. "What," I managed to mumble, "What can I do for you, Miss?"

"Misses." She flashed her brown eyes to catch my attention, and I felt her intensity. She was here on serious business, and I needed to pull myself together. "Murphy. Constance Murphy." She held her black leather purse close in front of her but let it go long enough to shake my hand. Soft and smooth. Fine leather smooth. Chiffon smooth. I absentmindedly rubbed my thumb and fingers together as I contemplated the delicious experience of touching her and the sweet scent that

5

accompanied her drawing near. It was deep purple and black, floral and vanilla. Sticky sweet like southern tea but with a squeeze of lemon. It flowed through me like a vapor. It swirled like a toke of smoke through my body and mind and I felt my lids settle again.

"Is this a bad time?"

"No. No." I took a deep breath. "I... just... need... coffee." Pushing against the desktop, I stood to a stoop and shuffled toward the coffee pot.

"I could come back." She started to turn, but I motioned sluggishly with an open hand for her to stay put.

"Gimme a minute." Guess it was no great surprise to her that I was a bit out of it. After all, I was damaged goods. Everyone in Louisville knew Jimmie Star was ruined. It was front page stuff.

I poured myself a cup and offered one to her, but she refused with a shake of her head. I took a long drink then turned back toward her to see the bright white flash from her left hand ring finger. It said happily married, but the tension in her face said otherwise.

"Now." I smiled. "Where were we?"

She studied me but didn't judge. Not that I could tell. To the contrary, I felt her care and concern, but she wasn't here to comfort me. I was supposed to help her, but all I could do was watch her hips swivel beneath the cream-colored coat as she took off her gloves. Her posture was proud but beat down. Her back was strong, but her shoulders slumped inward, and her head hung a bit. She was a lady, but she was tired, stressed out, and worn down.

"Please," I gestured toward the oak chair to her side, "have a seat."

She sat and made herself a compact form with legs crossed and arms clutching a Michael Kors handbag. Shiny black Steve Madden heels glistened at the ends of her smooth legs. I studied them for a moment, perhaps a bit too long, because she cleared her throat rather forcefully, and I responded by reaching for a box of Marlboro. I took out a smoke, raised it slowly to my lips, and flicked up a flame with my lighter. Drawing heavily on the cigarette, I watched the flame dance toward the end to ignite the dry tobacco. The hot smoke caressed the back of my throat, my chest expanded, and I exhaled a blue-grey cloud off to the side. "What can I do for you?"

Her white-tipped nails dug slightly into the leather of her purse. "I'm worried, Mr. Star." Her lips twitched. "I'm worried about a lady friend." The round edges of her teeth quickly scraped across her lower lip. "She's caught up in something." She bit her lip.

"Something?"

"Something dangerous."

I raised my brows, looked at her. That could be anything. This city crawled with dangers, and the possible scenarios of a woman in dire straits were too many to imagine without more information. I maintained my gaze, but she didn't speak. Instead she slowly unzipped her purse and

7

eased out an envelope, which scuffed against the metal teeth of the zipper to make a slight hissing sound. She opened the envelope, removed a few photographs, and slid them across my desktop. "Veronica Rene."

Getting down to business, I put on my glasses and looked at the photos. The images had been taken in low light, so they had that Technicolor psychedelic feel, but I could clearly see this dame was a looker. Blond hair hung down in swooping waves. Sparkling blue eyes with heavy lids. Flawless complexion.

"A beauty queen."

"Yes."

I rummaged around until I found a pen in my desk drawer. Then I scribbled in a small spiral notebook "Veronica Rene."

"Last name?"

"Don't know."

"Address?"

She shrugged, and her eyelids fluttered. She was holding out on me.

"Who is she?" The words flowed together seamlessly.

"A friend."

Anger flowed molten hot through my body. She was lying. "What kind of friend?" I clenched my teeth and gazed at her for a long moment, saw the artery in her neck pulse, and almost felt her heart thump.

"What kind of question is that?" She swept up the photos with a smooth movement, and my heart plummeted as though she had taken away my reason for being. I drew a quick breath as she put them back into the envelope. "You mean are we lovers, don't you?"

"Well, yes."

She huffed, and I felt my desperation grow. I needed this case. I needed her to trust me. I needed to be Jimmie Star again, and she knew that.

"I've gotta know what I'm gettin' into."

We stared at each other, and I tried to play it cool with a strong puff on my cigarette, but my hand shook. I was desperate to see those photos. I was desperate to be of service. I was desperate to play the hero. Again. She tossed the envelope back to the desktop. "Not lovers. Just friends. I'm worried about her. She's mixed up with some man. You may have heard of him. Name's Doc Laraunt."

A thousand cold needles pierced my spine, and I started to spiral into the pain and misery and fear that swirled around that name. Darkness descended around me as cold sweat beaded on my forehead. I bit my lip, rubbed a hand across my eyes, and took a deep breath. "Doc Laraunt?"

"Yes."

I nodded and continued nodding as the pressure built behind my eyes. I took a spastic breath and swallowed hard to fight back tears of rage and fear and regret. He was a destroyer, a despicable fiend and killer, and no man had ever ruined another man's life as he had ruined mine. I nodded. "Doc Laraunt?" A sudden twinge of pain caught me off guard, and I clutched a hand against my chest. "I can't." My voice trembled. "I can't."

"You're Jimmie Star?" Her brows knit. "Some tough guy." Smirking, she took her gloves from her pocket and began putting them on. "You had him. You had Laraunt dead to rights."

"Yeah." The pain swelled within my chest. It pressed against my ribcage until I thought my sternum would burst, so I jerked open my desk drawer to get some Oxi and heard the pills rattle in their brown plastic bottle. I took it in my hand, and, as I opened the top, she spoke her piece.

"Run to your pills. Run into your stupor, but know this. While you're doping yourself to high heaven, Veronica is in danger and her life is in your hands. You're the only one that can help her."

"Lady." I popped a few pills into my mouth and chased them down with a half shot of Four Roses left over from the night before. "You better find another--"

"I know what happened."

"Yeah." My brows pressed down. "You read about it." I glared at her. "I lived it." I picked up the framed photo from my desktop and turned it for her to see. "My wife." I swallowed hard. "She's dead. He killed her." I exhaled forcefully. "And the same bullet he shot through her heart is lodged next to mine."

She curled small in the chair across from me and shook as she sobbed, "I need to know she's alive." Desperation and anguish poured from her in a stream of tears, and my instinct was to take her into

10

my arms and hold her close. Instinct said comfort her and make everything alright, but I wasn't able at that moment to step up. Perhaps it was the salty scent of her tears that brought a flood of emotion I wasn't ready to deal with. Grief and fear and hatred mingled in a noxious stew that I'd have to eat sooner or later, but not then. I just couldn't. I couldn't accept the challenge. I couldn't feel my grief. I couldn't face my fear. I couldn't stay awake.

"Please, Jimmie." She walked to my side and clutched my head to her chest. "I know you've suffered. I know you're scared."

Her warm tears dripped on my neck, and something stirred deep inside me. Down below the yellow streak. An inkling of compassion and courage. Just enough for me to assure her that I'd find Veronica. Not enough to hold off sleep.

2

When I woke that evening Constance Murphy was gone, but the envelope lay on my desk. I noticed its sharp corners, yellow color and swollen center, and wondered what was inside. I gave it a catlike flick and watched it turn around its center. What would I find inside besides more trouble, more suffering, more Doc Laraunt? Hadn't I had enough of that man? He'd killed my wife and damn near killed me. I'd lost everything except my name, my degree, and the honorary key to the city. I saw it sticking out of a cardboard box filled with things I hadn't been able to part with. It was comically large and didn't open many doors these days. Nope. It seemed that as soon as the city leaders embraced me as a hero they turned their backs on me as a fallen, defeated, and shameful wretch. Well, fuck 'em. I was thunder before they ever heard me rumble and I was thunder still. A bit muffled and grumbling rather than awe-inspiring but I was thunder. Just needed to straighten up. That wasn't likely for as soon as I had that thought I pulled a bottle of Four Roses from my desk drawer, took a swig to chase down a couple pills, and lit up a smoke. I had a few problems. Yes. My way back from exile and alienation and despair would be crooked, but I would travel it to the end.

Taking the envelope in my hand, I noticed it was thicker than I recalled and heavy. Opening the clasp and flap, I tipped it to slide out the contents and was surprised when, in addition to the photos and a few other items, a stack of hundred dollar bills landed on my desktop. I looked at them, and a wave of relief spread through my body. I could finally pay my rent. Even a stack like this would not make a dent in my medical bills, but I could pay my rent and get some more medicine maybe even some Zanies too.

I stuffed three hundreds into my pants pocket then opened my desk drawer to slide the rest in on top of my snub-nosed Smith and Wesson. It felt good to have a pocket full of money and a meaty case. Perhaps I really could turn things around, get my feet under me, and make another go at living. First I'd need to find Veronica Rene.

I looked again at the photos. Veronica was stunning. Her blond hair flowed in a cascade of broad waves that rested on her shoulders. It framed her symmetrical face and covered her right eye. One of the photos had been taken at Churchill Downs. The second showed her in opulent surroundings of Greek columns with gilt capitols. The third was the most informative. Another selfie. This one had been taken in a mirror. I could see the phone. Top of the line iPhone. I could see something else. She held the device in her left hand, so I saw the flash and sparkle of a wedding ring. She was married. Where was her husband in all this? The fourth photo showed Veronica Rene standing at the railing on an upper floor of what appeared to be a hotel. Behind her the hollow space of the atrium and surrounding balconies identified the place as the Hyatt.

I reached for my Four Roses, took a strong pull straight from the bottle to finish it, and immediately realized I'd had a bit too much too fast. That drink combined with the pills hit me pretty hard. Sweat beaded on my face. My head grew heavy and lulled back. I snapped it back to vertical and, looking out onto the dusk street and the block buildings beyond, decided I'd had enough work for the day. I'd get a fresh start the next morning. That night, I trudged across the crumbling asphalt lot toward the Fog Light for more booze and some company. Along the way, I entered the only color on the grey expanse of Berry Boulevard. The purple and gold lights from the Fog Light lured me in.

What lay within was my new normal. Strippers. Bar girls. Drugs. This wasn't the quiet subdivision life I'd known before that night, nearly a year ago, when Laraunt had killed my wife. I was living in his world.

3

Walking through the door of the Fog Light, I paused for a few seconds to allow my eyes to adjust to the darkness. When they did, I saw Candy sitting close to me and leaning on a well-dressed middle-aged man. They were getting pretty chummy in the booth, and I didn't want to think about what might be happening beneath the table. Obviously, she was giving him the V.I.P. treatment: thirty dollars for thirty minutes.

Peaches saw me and approached right away.

"Jimmie." She smiled and took me by the elbow. "You sit here. Candy's a little busy but she'll be glad to see you." She led me to a high-backed booth. "Four Roses?"

"Yeah." When I sat, the exhausted seat gave way, and I felt like a child trying hard not to fall through a toilet seat.

"Right back."

I settled into the glow from the neon signs on the wall and studied the place. It hadn't changed in the six or so months I'd been going there, but I still liked to look around. It was all black and purple and chrome with a cosmic carpet of stars and galaxies on the floor and hard rock coming from the sound system. The video monitor showed lovely ladies, posed for my pleasure, and several ceiling-mounted fish-eye cameras recorded every shift of my eyes. Was someone watching? Someone other than the big fella standing near the bar?

I felt a light touch on my shoulder, a smooth stroke. Looking back, I saw purple-haired Candy walking toward the bar to fetch her V.I.P. a drink. She sparkled in a tight sequined dress, which clung to her thin waist, round bottom, and luxurious breasts. It was the body of a twenty-something and a great one at that. She looked across her shoulder and smiled. I loved her smile. Her weary smile. One day I would fall for her. One day, when I got myself together or fell apart completely.

Peaches set the drink on the table in front of me. "Where ya been, Jimmie?"

"Here and there." I laid a hundred on the table.

She smiled. "Guess so."

I watched her walk away. She was terribly skinny, and her skinny ass poked out of her skinny outfit, little more than straps and strips of black fabric. She looked like she'd been mauled by a tiger.

Wanting to save myself for Candy, I sipped my Roses and fiddled with the tiny straw from my glass. "Addicted to Love" came through the speakers, and I nodded my head slowly. Robert Palmer was a clever boy. No wonder he'd moved to Switzerland.

Just as the song ended, Candy slipped into the booth next to me, slid her hand across my thigh, and let it rest there. "Oh, Jimmie, when ya gonna take me away from here?"

I raised my brows, half smiled, then took a drink. A year ago, I'd never have considered such a proposition. I thought it was clear what she wanted from me.

Money. She would coo by my side so long as the money flowed. So long as I ordered drinks and tipped her well or went for the extras available in the Crystal Palace. My guard was up but it wasn't very strong or effective. I felt it waver when she settled against my arm and rubbed her cheek on my shoulder. It had been a long time since I'd lost Francesca. A long, lonely time. Candy sighed as she slid her hand up my leg. Some things are necessary in this life, and when I felt her grip on me, I knew what had to be done. She did too.

"Crystal Palace?"

The rush flowed through me. It was just that easy. Build a little trust. Lay down a little money. Enter into the sexual economy of Laraunt's world.

I finished my drink and took a few ice cubes in my mouth. "Yeah." I crunched the cubes. "Stop by the bar, babe. Get me a drink."

"You got it." She took the bill from the tabletop and headed for the bar.

I watched her walk, studied her sparkling bottom, shifting left and right. I imagined making love to her. That wasn't on the menu here. Had to go down the street for that. Hit the Derby City Lounge. Take a limo ride. She turned and showed me the drink. I slid out of the booth and looked at the glass block wall of the Crystal Palace. She walked that way, and I followed. She nearly disappeared in the bedazzling array of flashing lights from the glass blocks, but I managed to track her to the entrance.

When I reached her, she pressed herself against me, and I wrapped an arm around her waist to pull her gently toward me.

"Come on." She took my hand and led me inside, where we sat on a couch. She set my bourbon on a table and laid the change, a pile of small bills, beside it. The Crystal Palace costs forty dollars, so I figured there was about fifty left. I took a five from the stack and held it out for her. She smiled then took my hand to slide it under her skirt and up her thigh, where I tucked the bill into the band of her panties, and she pressed the back of my hand to keep it there on her supple thigh.

There are unwritten rules to such places. The first is that the girls are in charge. They are there to tease and titillate, and they are in charge of all touching. The second is you get what you pay for. Sometimes it's a chat at a table. Sometimes it's a little rub down in a booth. Other times, it's a visit to the privacy of the Crystal Palace. I was flush with cash and lonely so there I sat behind the glass wall with Candy, running her palm across my chest and breathing heavily on my neck. I felt my arousal: strong and urgent. I hadn't felt this way since the last time I was with her, and that had been a while.

She knew what I liked. She reached out for my drink and handed it to me. "Wanna stand up?" Like I said, she knew what I liked. I leaned forward, took the drink in my hand, and stood. When I did, she ran her hand up the inside of my thigh to

18

caress me. Then she stood and pressed herself against my back. I felt her breasts and her hot breath and her hands, sliding around to work my zipper. I took a long drink of thc Four Roses as she took me in her smooth hands and made me feel like a king.

4

I awoke to pain in my chest. The constriction and freezing pangs. As the anguish radiated through my body, I writhed on my couch. How I'd gotten there I didn't know. That was a question for another time. The good news was that I was home, and the medicine was nearby. Opening my eyes just enough to make out the medicine bottle on top of a cardboard box, I threw out my hand and clumsily grabbed it. I poured a few of the round pills into my palm and quickly swallowed them. It took only a couple minutes for the numbness to flow through me like molten chocolate over a cake. When the tormenting knot in my chest loosened just a little, I struggled to sit up on the edge of the couch, let out a long breath, and rub my eyes.

A single thought came to mind. Coffee. Black coffee in a cup. I needed it and thought about walking to the Castle on the corner but decided against the notion. Stiff and sore, I didn't want to be seen hobbling along the side of the street. I may have been washed up, but there was no point in advertising my decrepitude. Besides, I was making a comeback.

I went into the front room and started brewing a pot. While it brewed, I ran cold water from the faucet into my hands and splashed it on my face. When the coffeemaker gurgled, I poured a cup and carried it to the front door, where I stood and watched traffic and drank the java.

I spotted the envelope on my desk and thought of the money. Fearing I'd lost what I had on me, I thrust a hand into my pocket and pulled out two hundreds, a twenty, and a few fives. Good enough.

I walked to my desk and opened the drawer to see the crisp hundreds and my revolver. Everything was as I had left it. Now to work. I sat in the wooden chair, swiveled it to face the desk, and looked again at the photos of Veronica. She was all kinds of beautiful. Wavy blonde hair parted on her left and covering her right eye. Proud cheeks and flawless complexion. Veronica was most likely an assumed name. Just too cute.

I turned my attention to the other contents of the envelope. There was a smaller envelope. I set that aside so that I could savor the curiosity and checked out a piece of paper instead. It had Constance Murphy's information on it. Swanky Lake Forest address. Cell phone number. I'd start with this. First step of every investigation is to investigate the client. Gather a little background to see who I was dealing with. But first. There was the smaller envelope. I could no longer ignore it, so I ripped it open to find another photo, a handwritten letter signed Veronica, and a debit card with the personal identification number.

The photo was a 3 x 5 black and white. Like an actress's head shot. Couldn't tell where it had been taken, but Veronica was zooted. She was high as a kite and looked dynamite. All laid out on a bed, wavy blonde hair flowing smoothly around her symmetrical face. I licked my lips. Doc Laraunt? This girl had been turned out. But how? She was or had been a classy lady. Probably started as an escort, but her path was certain. A swift descent down the mountain of drugs and violence to the street.

Perhaps the letter would shed some light on her plight. It was addressed to Constance and had been written with a fountain pen. Judging by the ink, Mysterious Blue, it was a Waterman. For the most part, the script flowed smoothly, beautifully, and only wavered here and there. The letter itself indicated she was on the edge of her ability to cope with "certain circumstances." Knowing the company she kept, she meant drugs and alcohol. It was signed "Veronica" with flowing, almost lurid, swoops and curves. There was no indication of extreme nervousness, no excessive shakiness of line, just smooth, steady script. It didn't make sense. A personal letter between friends, a call for help that showed little distress in form or content. I set the letter aside and returned my attention to Constance. I still didn't know her relationship with Veronica.

A few keystrokes revealed Constance had graduated from the University of Louisville. An English major with good grades. Married Michael Murphy, and the couple moved into Lake Forest in 2006. Michael owned a restaurant and bar called the Mad Hatter in the Highlands. They had the usual mortgages and car payments. Like most Middletown folks, they were living on credit and the faith that his income would continue to pay the bills. They seemed typical enough, and I found no indication of deceit or harmful intent, so I started my search for Veronica in earnest.

An internet search on the name Veronica Rene turned up an advertisement for a local escort service, which listed Veronica Rene as "petite and vivacious with classic beauty." The ad featured a close up image of her wavy blond hair and provided a number to call for reservations. Easy enough. I'd call and request an evening with her. She would show up, and I'd judge for myself if she needed help. Hell, I might get a back rub. That would be nice.

Feeling certain I'd make quick work of this case, I picked up the handset and dialed the number. A woman answered, and I enquired about making reservations for an evening with Veronica. The woman said she hadn't been available for quite some time and recommended Connie as a comparable substitute.

"Had my heart set on Veronica."

"Sorry, but she's no longer with us. Connie is new. Very cute and sexy too."

"Any idea where I might find Veronica?"

"Can't say. Are you interested in Connie? I can send you a picture."

This woman was a dead end, but cute and sexy is a nice combination, and Connie may know something about Veronica.

"How 'bout tonight?"

"Oh, no. She's booking a few nights out." She worked the keyboard. "Looks like Friday."

"Okay. Dinner. Friday night."

We finalized the reservation for Friday. She would meet me at the Mad Hatter. Might as well get a look at the place.

It was getting near noon, and I was hungry, so I strapped on my shoulder holster, slipped my pistol in it, and put on my sports coat. I put the photos in the inside pocket and headed to O'Bryan's for a working lunch.

It was a bit of a drive down Dixie Highway, but they had the best oysters in town. I knew the owner. Hell of a nice guy. He knew all the goings on around town. Perhaps he would know a thing or two about where the pictures had been taken.

5

When I merged from Old Seventh Street onto Dixie Highway south and passed under the Watterson Expressway, I felt the shift of environment, mood, and class. Berry Boulevard and Seventh Street were all about cheap car batteries and cheaper women. Dixie was all about car lots, chain restaurants, and funeral homes. The whole place felt like a small southern town, sitting at the base of the tall hills to the east. It still had a few mom and pop shops and small town motels where the men backed their trucks in to conceal their plates, but it was burgeoning with new, fancy places to buy a five dollar coffee or a six dollar burrito. Not pretty, but it beat the industrial feel of Berry Boulevard.

We had lived here in Pleasure Ridge Park. Me and Francesca. A cozy brick job in a green subdivision a mile west of Dixie. I guess it was nice enough. I never wanted a big shiny life. I just wanted intensity. I wanted to be consumed and engrossed with passion. That meant work. Investigating. Discovering. Dodging danger. The brick box in Fiddler's Heights wasn't the setting for drama. It was home. Quiet. Peaceful.

She worked at the University of Louisville in the Languages Department, and I had an office in a building on Bardstown Road. Things were going well enough, and we were renovating the place by littles. New furnace and A.C. New water heater. I poured a concrete patio out front and surrounded it with boxwoods for a sense of privacy. We would sit there in the evenings to watch the walkers make their rounds, fast and slow. We would wave and smile and they would too. Francesca hung feeders for the hummingbirds, and each spring we awaited their arrival. It wasn't the American dream of rapid advancement but it was a good life for me and a tolerable one for her. She had grown up in Switzerland and was accustomed to more luxury than I could afford. Still, she didn't seem to suffer much.

We met at U of L, while she was doing her study abroad, and she was the answer to my prayers. Following my breakup with my high school sweetheart, Leslie, and a few purely sexual relationships, I had given up on finding a beautiful girl with her intellectual curiosity and moral decency intact. I gave up all pursuit of women and focused on studies. Despite being lonely, I was doing well. Pursuing a Masters in Humanities through the week and working odd jobs on the weekends.

Then Francesca walked into the Humanities Building. She looked lost, and I broke from my usual hide-and-watch mode to walk up to her. I couldn't understand her very well, due to her accent, but we managed to establish that we had two courses in common. Rhetoric and Philosophy of Language. Those two classes served as the stepping stones for our romance until her return home to finish her training as a translator. I visited her on breaks from school, and we exchanged letters and the occasional phone call, until our long-distance relationship culminated in marriage.

Her father staked our purchase of the Fiddler's Heights place, and we set to homemaking. She went to work at the university while I finished my graduate degree. After becoming disillusioned with academic life, I cast about for a line of work that offered freedom and excitement and decided to become a private investigator. I got my P.I. license and my first piece. A hammerless Smith and Wesson 38 Special. Compact and easy to draw. I felt it in my shoulder holster as I passed a car dealership on the right and turned down Flintlock Road.

I pulled my dusty Ranger into a space at O'Bryan's pub and walked past the humming window unit sticking out from the block wall to push through the door. The place was just as I remembered. Well-lit with sunlight from several windows. Blue and white. U of K all the way. I sat on a tall stool at a round table in the bar area, and the bartender, wearing a hat that said "happy happy happy," asked what I was drinking. I called for a beer, and quick as an owl shits she handed me one with ice on the bottle. I ordered pan fried oysters and watched her pass through the shiny metal door into the kitchen. Sitting at the table, I looked around the place. There were Christmas lights arranged in neat rows on the white tile ceiling. They didn't blink or cause any distraction. They just glowed happily. The L-shaped, wood-topped bar ran for thirty feet or more, and at half past noon there were about eight men in their late forties and older sitting at the bar and at round tables like mine. They were all big men. Burly. Strong. Wearing ball caps. One man wore an outfit of mismatched camouflage. Part army issue. Part oak pattern. Two men to my right were drinking beers from buckets and talking. I started on my beer as another big man in his fifties sat down at the bar.

"Hey, Bob."

"Yeah."

"You know Pup, don't you?"

"Yeah."

"I was just tellin' him how you used to work for the beer distributor and how you used to toss around those kegs like they was nothin'."

Bob chuckled. "Long time ago, Ken."

"For you and me both."

Bob laughed.

"What's in a keg? Twelve gallons?"

"Fifteen and a half."

"How many twelve ounce cups ya get from that?"

"One hundred eighty-five."

Finishing my beer, I laughed with amazement at the number and his knowledge of it." I showed Ms. Happy my empty and she reached into the cooler for a full one.

"And what's a keg weigh?"

"Hundred sixty-one pounds."

Ken turned to Pup. "See." He smiled. "That's a man. Tossing those kegs around two at a time."

"No doubt."

When I had rubbed the ice off my bottle, the oysters arrived. Beautiful brown lumps sitting in a paper boat. I took a long swig of my cold brew and tried to ignore them until they cooled enough to eat.

Pup and Ken got a bit loud at this point. They were establishing their bragging rights regarding their humble beginnings.

"Twenty-fifth and Dunkin. Portland." Ken exclaimed. "That's where I started." He finished his beer. "Look at me now. I'm doin' alright. Been with Ford twenty years." He grabbed another beer from the bucket. "Livin' in Raven's Point, and I got rental property."

About this time, John, the owner, walked from the back of the house. He smiled when he saw me, and I nodded. I figured the oysters were cool enough to eat, so I picked one up and bit into the crust, which gave way to the smooth, rich oyster within. Delicious would be an understatement. Those things were beyond mere food to be absentmindedly consumed. They were works of art to be savored, and that's what I did. I savored each juicy morsel then finished my beer just as Pup and Ken started debating who was going to pay for their buckets.

"Add 'em up, honey." Pup called out to Ms. Happy. "I got it." He walked to the bar with a handful of money. "Give one to everyone." He turned around, and I gave him a smile. I had decided to stop drinking but there was one oyster left in the little paper boat, so this freebee came just in time. I stepped to the bar and collected it. On my way back to the table, I stopped to thank Pup, and we shook hands for a long time. It was a bit of communion between daylight drinkers. Something those that drink only by the light of the moon know nothing about.

I took my last oyster and fresh brew over to join John at the bar.

"Hey, Jimmie."

"Good ta see ya, John."

"Place aint the same without ya."

"Yeah." I half smiled. "Been a while. I'm out on Berry Boulevard now." I bit into the oyster. "Nothing like this out there."

"Yeah. Been by your place a time or two." He nodded. "How ya been?"

"So so." I pulled the pictures from my jacket pocket. "Know this girl?"

He raised his brows and whistled. "You kiddin'?" He shook his head. "Way outta my league."

"Mine too." I smiled. "Can ya tell me where this one was taken? The one with the columns?"

He looked at it and licked his lips. "I bet it was that fancy hotel in Indiana. The one they redid a few years back. Hey, Pup!"

"Yeah."

"What's the name of that fancy place up in French Lick? Got the big dome."

"West Haden."

"Yeah." John pointed to Pup. "That's it."

"West Haden?"

"Yeah. Old place. Some quack built it long time ago, tryin' to attract tourists to the stinky water for healin'." He laughed. "Not too far." John leaned in. "You on a hot case?"

"Missing person."

"I'd sure miss her."

I finished my beer and put a twenty on the bar. "Thanks, John."

"Listen," he whispered, "how's it feel to know Laraunt is walking free?"

I swallowed hard and my hand sprang to my chest to cover the scar.

"I mean after what he did to you?"

Blood rushed to my face, and I sat silent for a moment.

"I don't wanna put you on the spot."

"Well." I gripped the edge of the bar. "It's hard."

"Yeah."

Just then Mrs. Happy opened the metal door, and I saw myself in its reflection. A handsome man with dark hair gone grey on the sides, salt and pepper beard, and bloodshot eyes, glimmering with the vague but growing desire for vengeance.

***

The day was still young, and West Haden was only an hour away, so I decided to visit the hotel to see what or who I would find. I thought for a moment of swinging by the Fog Light to see if Candy wanted to ride along. I'd heard the place was really fantastic and figured she might enjoy seeing it. I puzzled at the thought. We weren't close like that, but somehow I found myself thinking of her more and more.

6

Westbound Watterson past Dixie dove deep into poverty. Off the side of the elevated expressway I saw roofs with blue tarps spread over them, overgrown lawns, cinderblock buildings with bars on the windows and hand-painted signs on the walls. Al's Liquor caught my eye, and I thought of pulling off the expressway for a bottle to keep me company. I kept driving. Never know what could happen in a place like that. Might interrupt a dice game or be interrupted by some desperate drunk or drug-addled hood rat with a gun and the strong urge to use it. Growing more uncomfortable with the abandoned cars on the side of the road and the looming billboard advertisements for liquor, I clenched my teeth and kept driving. Merging onto 64 west, I started across the Sherman Minton Bridge. The rapidly changing geometric patterns created by the steel beams and vertical suspension cables captured my attention and soothed my nerves. I drew a deep breath, shifting my gaze to the tree-covered hills of southern Indiana, and felt my body relax. I was free of the city. Free from the noise and clutter. The trash and sideways glances. I was passing New Albany and headed for the country.

Just over the second hill, I exited onto 150 and stayed on it until I reached the Paoli town square just outside French Lick. It was a wide swath of asphalt around the grounds of the high-pillared town hall. Arranged along the points of a compass and situated on the sloping crest of a hill, the sides of the square were lined with staggered two and three story brick buildings that formed the core of the business district. There were secondhand clothing and antique shops, a propane dealer, a hotel, and a pub, situated between a barber shop and a law office. It seemed like a sweet spot for some scuttlebutt, so I stopped in for a snoop.

Stepping from my Ranger, I noticed the air was much fresher and crisper here than in town. It was significantly less humid and free of the noise, exhaust fumes, and generally bad vibes of the city. Straightening my clothes and stretching my stiff muscles as I went, I strolled across the sidewalk toward the front door. Entering, I noticed the smell of beer and wood. Not a bad combination. The place was narrow and deep, and the yellow pine-topped bar on my right was overhung with straw or some other dry grassy stuff to give it an island feel. The walls were paneled with slabs of wood, running vertically. There were four people sitting at the bar. Three guys. One lady. Jeans. Tee shirts. Ball caps. Tattoos. They were chatting and laughing. No one was dangerously drunk. I walked across the oak floor, sat on a black wood stool, and looked at the mirror-backed display of shiny glass bottles filled with liquors of various colors.

The bartender wiped a glass clean while he chatted with the group of drinkers. He looked my way, and I flashed my index finger. He sat down the glass he had been polishing and patted the bar top with an open hand to excuse himself from the group.

"What'll it be?"

"Four Roses. Rocks."

I watched him work and liked his style. Nothing fancy. Moving with smooth efficiency, he gathered up the ice with a metal scoop, dropped it in the glass, and poured the liquor. The only flare he exhibited was to raise the bottle away from the glass just a little before he stopped pouring so that a stream of golden brown nectar glistened in midair.

He took a square paper napkin from a small stack, flipped it over with a flick of his wrist, and set it down in front of me. Then he clunked the drink down on it.

"Roses and rocks."

I tossed a ten toward him. He picked it off the yellow bar top and walked to the old fashioned cash register. Watching him work the round keys reminded me of typing on my father's old typewriter. As a kid, I'd written stories on it. Monsters. Ladies in distress. Heroes coming to the rescue. Stuff like that. Perhaps it was those youthful fantasies and the desire to be a hero that inspired me to become a private detective, but I soon learned the job wasn't very glamorous or heroic. Sure, I'd taken down the mayor and had been slated to testify against Louisville's criminal elite, but there is nothing

35

uplifting about holding your dying wife until you collapse from the same bullet that took her down. We laid on that dark sidewalk like a pile of blood-soaked clothes until the police and ambulance arrived to take us away. I survived, but for what? To endure the pain in my heart and trudge on without her?

The bartender laid five ones on the bar in front of me, and I smiled a little. Everyone is scheming. He turned to walk away, but I stopped him. "Hey, buddy."

He turned. "Yeah?"

I licked my lips. "What ya know about West Haden?"

"The hotel?" He raised his brows. "What's to know?" He shrugged. "Up the road a bit. Old place with an awesome dome."

I pushed the stack of ones to him. "Anything go on up there?"

He cocked his head to the side a bit and looked at me from the corner of his eye. "Like what?"

"Like girls." I dug into my pocket for more small bills.

"Girls?"

"Yeah." I raised my brows. "You know. Tits and such."

I guess I had pushed him too hard, because he smirked and started to turn.

"Hold on." I set a twenty on the bar to regain his attention then pulled the photos from my jacket pocket. "Maybe you've seen this one around." I set them on the bar top.

He picked up the pictures and his eyes sprang open.

"Yeah." I nodded. "A hot one."

He shook his head, licked his lips slowly, and spoke quietly. "Well, if you're lookin' for her at the hotel, I'd be surprised if she wasn't with—" He glanced at the twenty in my hand, and I dropped it to the bar. "Word is a lady's man named Laraunt stays up there."

The blood drained from my face, dizziness descended upon me, and I had to take hold of the bar top to keep from falling off the stool. My stomach churned like a concrete mixer slopping the oysters and beer and bourbon and pills until my mouth filled with saliva, and I had to close my eyes and swallow hard to prevent myself from vomiting.

"You okay?"

I couldn't speak. I just pressed my lips together, squeezed my eyelids shut, and nodded slowly. But I wasn't okay. I was in bad shape and getting worse. Sweat beaded on my forehead, and the energy drained from my torso like someone had pulled the plug on a bathtub to send the hot water swirling in a nauseating whirlpool. My heart beat hard, and the pain grew steadily until I couldn't sit still. I had to get outta there. Against the barkeep's protests, I slid from the stool and stumbled toward the door. Pushing through it into the light of the square, I looked left and right. He could be anywhere. Waiting. Watching. I went straight to my truck and, feeling my heart thump painfully, tore off the way I'd come.

I swerved down 150. Breathing heavily, I sped through Chambersburg, where the road turns curvy. My body tingled with, well, what else would it have been? My body tingled with fear. I gripped the wheel and didn't slow for five minutes. When I reached the five or six buildings that form the town of Rego, I let off the gas and eased to the side of the road.

Pain seared my heart, so I pulled a few Oxi pills from my pocket and swallowed them. Then I waited. Wiping sweat from my face, I checked the rearview. Nothing there except the winding road, leading back to Paoli and, beyond that town, on the horizon, the dome of West Haden.

7

By the time I reached 64 east, my breathing and heartrate had returned to normal, but emotionally I was still a mess. I wanted Francesca. I wanted to lay in her arms, feel her fingers run through my hair until I fell asleep. It had been nearly a year. The wound in my chest had healed into a knotty purple and white scar. The doctors hadn't cut me much. Said the bullet was too close to my heart, and getting it would have required at least the removal of some ribs, so they just stopped the bleeding and sewed me up. The bullet was still there. A cold lump pressing heavily upon the very center of my being.

★★

We had been celebrating that evening. The deputy mayor had given me the key to the city for exposing the mayor's corruption. I stood on the steps of the Hall of Justice along with local dignitaries, as he spoke of my selfless deeds, courage, and tenacity. I looked into the small audience, past the row of picture-snapping newspaper guys, to find Francesca in her grey pea coat. She smiled and her eyes beamed with pride. We were making it. This honor wasn't about wealth or fame. It was about appreciation and acceptance. It was the city's way of taking me into its arms.

After the ceremony and the handshaking merry-go-round, I met Francesca at The Oak Table for dinner. It was out of our league but within our reach to celebrate this occasion. It wasn't every day the city embraced you publicly, and we wanted to savor the moment. We sat at a small square table by one of the large half-circle windows. The walls were paneled in dark oak with intricate scroll work around the windows. Hanging from the oak-beamed ceiling, an ornate brass chandelier with several frosted glass globes cast delicate light on our sparkling glassware and white tablecloth. The gentle sounds of private conversations murmured through the room to create a mesmerizing drone, accented by the occasional laugh or clink of silverware on china.

As the setting sun glinted on the first flakes of snow, we chatted, and our eyes met. She was beautiful. Her eyes sparkled with every brilliant reflection from the table. They captivated me. Looking into them, I drew a deep breath and sighed my complete contentment. I reached across the table, took her hand in mine, and smiled gently. I didn't have to tell her I loved her. She knew.

After dinner and dessert, I walked Francesca to her car. Snow fell quickly to blanket the city and give it the appearance of an ink painting in progress. A dark expanse of black night stretched across the top from corner to corner, and, beneath a streetlamp, we stood in a washed out off-white sketch. Just a few lines and slight variations of value indicated corners and edges of tall buildings. I was a little drunk, and her smile sparkled and glistened beneath the harsh white light. We embraced, and I closed my eyes to feel her love, warm and tingly. When I opened them, I saw him. A dark figure extending his right hand and taking one long step toward her from behind. I looked at his face. It was Doc Laraunt. Francesca jolted in my arms as a loud boom crackled in my ears until it resolved into a high-pitched ringing tone. She died instantly, and I stood, holding her limp body. Her head hung to the side, and I struggled to look into her face. I didn't understand what had happened. Didn't comprehend anything except her heavy limpness and my bewildered tears. Growing aware of the harsh pain in my chest and warm flow of blood, I held her until I grew too weak, and we fell into the white snow.

8

Back on Berry Boulevard, I pulled into the lot at my office and walked across the street to Classy Liquors for a bottle and a pack of smokes. When I pushed through the door I smelled alcohol. High proof stuff. Seems there had been an incident. The clerk had moments before interrupted a shoplifter in the vodka section. They scuffled, and to cover his escape the would-be-thief knocked a dozen bottles to the floor before running for the door.

The place was a mess, but the clerks let me in. "Watch the glass." Staying clear of the jagged shards and the pool of vodka, I picked up a fifth and a little pecan pie. All was going well until I went to check out. The cashier was on edge. Flashed his eyes at me with bad intentions and fidgeted with his hands when I asked him for a pack of smokes. Must've been hyped up on testosterone and energy drinks. I saw the angular form of a pistol in his front pocket, and a chill ran through me, so I got out of there.

Crossing the street, I looked at the purple and yellow lights from the Fog Light. I was hungry and wanted to go in for a bite and a chat with Candy if she was working, but first I wanted to read the paper and have a drink. I pulled my keys from my pocket and worked the deadbolt on my office door. Letting myself in, I noticed the stale smell of the place. It wasn't moldy. Just not homelike. No dog came running, and no one called out from the next room. Just a linoleum tile floor, painted block walls, and a few boxes of things I hadn't been able to part with just yet. Vestiges of that life I'd once lived with Francesca.

I sat at my desk and pulled the small spiral-bound notebook from my pocket. I opened it and wrote "West Haden = Doc Laraunt" and drew a circle around the words. I tossed the notebook on the desktop, opened the pie, and bit into it. The flaky crust crumbled, and the gooey filling spread sticky sweet across my tongue. I chewed on the dense pecans, and chased the thing down with a bit of cold coffee. Cracking open the Roses, I smelled the floral bouquet of the amber liquor, poured a shot in the now empty coffee cup, and gulped it down.

I felt funky and smelled a little ripe. Couldn't see Candy like that, so I decided to go to the Dixie Motel for a shower. We had a deal. Me and the manager. From time to time, they would call me to clear out some deadbeats. I'd let myself in and roust the losers toward the door. Occasionally one of them would buck up, but all it took was a flash of my piece to get him stepping. In return, I'd get a room when I needed it. Didn't need a reservation. Just show up. The place rented by the hour. I tossed back another shot and gathered some clean clothes and razor and such from the back room.

Leaving my office, I saw Candy walking to her car and called out to her. She looked my way and smiled.

9

She wore a rhinestone-studded black dress that sparkled beneath the streetlamp. Aglitter like a fairy or a ghost, she captivated me, and I fell under the sway of her seemingly supernatural presence. I couldn't keep my eyes off of her soft curves. Her round bottom and breasts. Her shiny legs. I wanted some time with her but wasn't sure how she would react if I made a move. This wasn't work. She had made her money for the day.

She swayed gently while we chatted, and each slight shift of position revealed new, dazzling stars and curves, and I found myself thinking of the constellations overhead, the vastness of the universe, and the intimacy of small spaces. A deep, gnawing desire brought my body to life with intense sensations. Tingling. Burning. Throbbing.

How could I ever think she would be interested in me? A middle-aged, washed-up detective. I was lucky she even spoke to me without the obligation of work, without the structured roles of client and service provider. What was I thinking?

I listened as she spoke in a lilting-sweet voice, and thrills traveled my spine to spread through my body. I desired her more than I ever had within the purple and black and chrome confines of the Fog Light. My heartbeat turned jazzy. It was do or die. I rubbed my fingers against my thumb. Looking at the roundness of her cheek, I started to raise my hand, but fear checked the movement. She was my closest friend. She listened to my secrets and didn't judge, but that was work.

Watching her glistening mouth move as she spoke, I chewed my lip, drew a deep breath, and reached out to stroke her cheek with my fingertips.

"Listen." I hesitated. "I'm headed out. Wanna join me?"

She leaned her head to the side. It was just a moment, but in that moment, I regretted what I had done. How could I show my face in the Fog Light again? How could I chat her up so casually now that she knew there was more than a few bucks at stake. My heart was on the line. I waited while she pondered my proposition then smiled, and nodded.

"Great." My shoulders relaxed. "My truck's over here." I took her by the elbow, and we walked the short distance to my Ranger.

"Gotta stop by a friend's first."

"Hop in." I opened the passenger door and watched her step up into the cab. Her smooth legs shined, and I imagined feeling her supple flesh off the clock.

"Just across Berry. Lentz Avenue."

"Sure thing." I revved the engine, released the clutch, and got under way. Where we were going, I didn't know. She was navigating, and I was happy to follow her directions.

"Turn right here. Down a block or so. On the left." I drove slowly until I came to a single story clapboard house painted Wildcat blue. "Stop here. Be right back."

I pulled next to the curb. She opened the door, stepped out, trotted up the sidewalk, and climbed the few steps of the porch to the front door. She knocked. A tall man wearing a bath robe answered. He looked at me and spoke to Candy. He looked again then let her in. This was a drug buy. I knew that. I just didn't know what the drug was.

Waiting in the truck, I ran my tongue across my teeth and felt the gritty film on their flat surfaces, so I looked in the console for a napkin. When I found one, I used it to polish my teeth. I also found a ketchup packet, which I squeezed into my mouth to freshen my breath. There was nothing I could do about the body funk. I'd just have to wait for the shower at the Dixie Motel.

I turned on the radio and went through the stations to find some music Candy might like. They played hard rock in the club, but I thought that was not her personal style. What kind of music would she like? I found a pop station and, though it made my skin crawl, left it there.

I was suffering through the caterwauling of some auto-tune songstress when I heard Candy laugh from the porch. I looked across my shoulder to see her lean into the man. They shared a little hug, which had more the air of ceremony than genuine feeling, then she turned and walked toward the road and me and everything that lay ahead. She opened the door, got in.

"You get high?"

"Sure."

"Let's go to the park." She smiled. "Overlook."

"I need to clean up."

"You're fine."

I drove down Taylor Boulevard toward the park, and my heart thumped with the uncertainty of what lay ahead and in time with the pop tune on my radio, as I imagined kissing her sweetly but passionately. I would take her into my arms beneath the stars and moon and—

"What's this?" She managed between laughs.

"What?"

"On your radio? Is that techno?"

"Hell. I don't know. Thought you might like it."

"Lord, no." She smiled. "Put on some Zeppelin."

I hit number one on the presets, and we grooved to the classics.

The road to the overlook was closed, so I parked in the small parking lot by the gate. She pulled a sack of weed from her sequined clutch. I watched her load a paper with sticky green and roll it up nice and tidy. She put the dope back into her purse, popped open her door, and stepped out.

"Ready?" She gestured to the sky. "Great place to smoke." She closed the door and started walking. I followed her up the road into the oak forest, and she fired up the joint. When she hit it, the cherry glowed bright red to illuminate her almond-shaped face. Something about her eyes fascinated me. They dipped down near her nose to give her a vaguely oriental look. She held out the joint for me to take, and I rubbed her fingertips when I did. I took a long toke, held the smoke as long as possible, and let it out in a smooth stream of grey, moonlit vapor. It quickly took hold, and everything became more of what it was. The darkness of the road became darker, and the dry leaves on the trees rustled in a soft melody against the rhythmic song of tree frogs. Our footsteps fell into unison, and we entered into nature and reality.

She passed the joint back to me, and I took another drag.

"You know what I miss this time of year?" Her smooth voice slipped into my awareness like a soft breeze flowing through me.

I raised my brows, let smoke pass through my lips, and then said, "What's that?"

"June bugs."

"June bugs?"

"Yeah."

We walked. Side by side. She was small. Not petite like Constance. Just smallish. Dark purple hair cut to her shoulders. Round and smooth. Curvy. I licked my lips and felt my arousal. The tree frogs' song hummed through my body. Deep inside, it coursed through me. Tingled. Thrilled. Healed. "June bugs?"

"Yeah. Big shiny beetles."

"Why are they called June bugs?"

"They come in June. Up from the ground. They're really big. Size of a nickel or quarter." She showed me the size with a space between her thumb and index finger. For a moment I thought she was holding something. Something I couldn't see. I looked at it. The empty space in her grasp. Moonlight winnowed through the canopy to make her dress glisten and sparkle, and I fell under her spell. I was captivated. What was she holding? What was she offering me?

"June bugs." She reminded me. "We used to catch 'em. Fill up Mason jars with 'em." She smiled, and a thrill ran through my body. "Tie a thread to their legs."

I looked at her curiously.

"They fly."

I imagined her with a bunch of June bugs flying around her. Buzzing. Circling. Her at the center. Sparkling and offering something invisible. "Oh."

"They're so pretty. Smooth and shiny. And they have tiny little heads on big ol' bodies." She laughed a bit. "And their legs are really scary. All spikey. But they're harmless." She tilted her head to the side and smiled. "What kinda bugs did you play with?"

The answer came immediately to mind. "Praying mantis."

"Scary." She held up her hands to mimic a mantis pose.

"Yeah." I raised my brows. "Guess so."

"They eat baby hummingbirds."

"Really?"

"Yeah." She licked her lips, and her eyes grew large. "Rip 'em to bits and chew 'em up."

A dark feeling came over me. It echoed the darkness of the road we were walking. Up. Up. It curved with the contours of the hill. Through the dark woods toward the peak. We fell silent for a while. Just listened to the frogs and crickets and our footsteps. My desire for her grew stronger. I hadn't felt this way in years. Perhaps ever. Sure, she worked in a gentlemen's club. Chatted up lonely geezers and jacked off desperate fools such as myself, but that was work. Everyone has to make a living.

We kept climbing until the road turned right and leveled. We were at the peak and headed through the dark forest toward the lookout. We were breathing heavily, and I had worked up a little sweat. Ahead, the road opened up to reveal the sparkling lights of downtown in the distance. We walked into the opening. Beneath the stars and moon. A wave of joy flowed through my body as light filled my vision, and I turned to her, sparkling like a bit of the night sky by my side.

Deep into the night, we sat side by side, smoking, talking, and watching the city glow in the distance. I wanted to kiss her, but she clung to my arm in such a way that I couldn't lean in to make a move. She was blocking me, even as she clung to me. She was in control, and I respected that. She needed a friend, someone to relate to, and I was that friend. After all, we were both damaged goods.

She had had a difficult childhood. Her drunken father had abused her. Physically. Emotionally. Sexually. Then as a young adult, she'd been raped. The rapist had been an acquaintance, and he had sent her life careening off course. She had ambitions to attend college, but the emotional turmoil caused her to fail her senior year of high school. More than the rape itself, the torment of being blamed and shamed for the deed had left a deep wound in her psyche. I think that's why she worked at the club. She wanted to have power over men. Make them want her without being able to have her. That was a dangerous game. In the club there was the big bouncer to handle anyone who got out of line, but outside in the world, she was on her own and vulnerable.

She pressed against my shoulder and clung to my arm. I wanted to fondle her breasts and bury myself in her, but she was lonely and desperate for companionship. Again, I was called upon to be the hero. Nodding, I consigned myself to my role. I imagined seeing us from above. Two people, side by side, sitting on the highest point in the city. It was a sacred moment, and everything was okay. Everything was as it should be.

We watched the sun rise pastel pink, and then walked back down the hill to my truck. We held hands on the way, and I asked, "You ever wonder where a thought comes from?" She raised her brows. "I mean." I licked my lips and swallowed hard. "They manipulate us. Feed us images and messages through the media. Project Mockingbird. The government twists us up in tight little knots of hate and greed. They feed us thoughts and feelings and attitudes. Whatever suits them. Mostly hate and greed."

"I know what you mean." She half smiled. "They set us against each other, especially men against women."

"Yeah. And it starts so early, and the messages are so pervasive. When I was about seventeen, I was living in some rundown apartment my father rented for me on Gagle Avenue. I decided to trace down the source of every thought and root out the false ones, the ones that hadn't come from my own thinking."

"Sounds difficult. I mean, we get thoughts from reading and radio and TV and preachers and a thousand other places. It's all brainwashing."

"Yeah."

"How did you do it?"

"Everything I said or thought I asked myself 'where did that come from?' Turns out a lot of my thoughts were song lyrics and commercial jingles." I laughed. "Some are things my father and mother said. I rejected them all. I wanted to know what *I* thought."

"What happened?"

"I destroyed myself. Perhaps it was my false self. I looked into the abyss of naked anxiety and sank deep into it. I remember I had these two doves that my girlfriend at the time had given me. They had gotten out of their cage, and they terrified me. They took over the apartment, and I locked myself in the bedroom. When I heard them cooing in the living room, my heart went crazy, and I hid beneath the covers."

"So what happened?"

"After a while, my father came over to check on me. He found me on the bed, probably crying. He freaked out about the birds and made me get up."

"What did you learn?"

"Turns out I didn't think anything at all. Once I liberated myself from the echo chamber of false thoughts, I decided I could only trust direct experience. The sun on my skin is warm. Always is. It doesn't lie. It doesn't depend on my perspective or interpretation or mood. Reality. Seeing the world as it is. That is truth."

"Guess so."

"And something interesting happened. Over time, I developed a kind of sixth sense. Every experience gives rise to an emotion. This is not reason. This is not mathematics. This is direct experience. And this is what I gained by rejecting the false self."

She took my hand in hers. I felt the smooth softness of her skin, and a sudden quiver of my chin surprised me. I bit my lip lightly, as I opened the door for her. Again, I looked at her shiny legs when she stepped into the truck.

We were quiet on the ride back to the Fog Light, but when I dropped her off, she kissed me quickly and said, "My name is Mary."

With that, the utterance of her given name, everything changed between us. She had revealed herself. We were friends and headed for something more intimate. There would be no more hand jobs in the Crystal Palace. Our relationship no longer involved a cash economy. From that point on, love was our currency. Love and heroin.

11

I opened the door of the room in the Dixie Motel and smelled bleach. My eyes watered a bit as I walked to the bed. The mattress, covered with a floral print polyester spread, compressed flimsily when I sat on it. I was tired. I was grimy. I was ready for a shower and coffee. Starting the pot, I headed to the small, porcelain and plastic bathroom. It smelled like someone had poured a gallon of bleach out in there. At least they kept the place clean. I hung my shoulder holster from a hook on the wall, undressed, and rubbed a hand across my small belly. Turning the plastic knobs, I started the water in the shower. I pulled shaving gear and a toothbrush from my duffle, started hot water in the sink, and brushed my teeth. When the water ran hot, I warmed the blades of my razor and shaved my neck up to my beard. I looked at it, framing my face, and nodded. It was nice. Manly.

I stepped over the side of the tub and entered the stream from the shower head. The water was very hot, and I flinched but assured myself that I would get used to it. Soon my discomfort gave way to relaxation and enjoyment.

I used the motel's shampoo. It had a smell with no particular referent. Neither floral nor perky nor manly. It was just a smell. I massaged the shampoo through my thinning hair and beard, then leaned my head back to let the water flow over my face, and my mind drifted to my evening with Mary. She was playing a dangerous game. In the club, she was so close to danger yet mistook it for safety. The image of Veronica flashed through my mind. Her wavy blond hair flowed and undulated through my imagination before giving way to the image of Constance, weeping in my office. Broken by the plight of a friend. I had to get on task. Had to find Veronica Rene. Tonight I would meet Connie at the Mad Hatter. Maybe she could point me in the right direction.

12

The Highlands proper is a few blocks on Bardstown Road that constitute a hipster paradise. Microbreweries. Record, video, and game shops. Vintage clothing stores. In my U of L days it was all dumps and dives but the only hangout for college kids. Now, it was growing up. There were big chain places with that funky feel by design. A few of the old places were still around, but Ear X-tacy music store had closed a while back. When it did, I lost interest and stopped making the promenade. It was doing fine without me.

The Mad Hatter was just starting to fill up with college kids grooving to loudish alternative rock, which wasn't bad but annoyed me when it strayed too far from the tones and rhythms of the classics. I looked around. The front room was a large oak-floored square with the bar running along the back. Televisions on the walls played "Alice in Wonderland." The Johnny Depp version.

I made my way between dark wood tables and chairs to a few steps to the right of the bar. They led to a hallway with the restrooms on the right and kitchen on the left. There was a large service window that gave access to the kitchen. At the end of the hall was another large room with pool tables. Probably the same ones I'd played on twenty years earlier. I looked around. Nothing nostalgic. It was just a building with a name out front.

Walking back toward the bar, I passed the kitchen window on my right. Through it I noticed a smallish, well-groomed man with thin lips and dark hair parted on the side. He wore a sports coat and striped club tie, which indicated to me he was most likely the owner, Michael Murphy. Who else would be in a pizza kitchen wearing a sports coat? Well, my assumption was quickly proven wrong. There was a second man wearing a sports coat in the kitchen. He was large, taller than the first by several inches, and thick-bodied. I recognized him. Sal Lucca. One of Laraunt's crew.

I ducked into the men's room across the hall and, holding the door open just a smidge, watched the two men. Sal was putting the screws to Michael. He was in his space, and Michael was backing away. When Michael could back no farther, Sal leaned into his face and said, "You will do this for me." Murphy nodded.

Sal gave him a firm pat on the cheek and turned away. "Expect a truck tonight."

Lucca had his fingers in lots of pies, and the Mad Hatter was one of them. Like it or not, Murphy had a partner, and this partner had turned him from businessman to criminal. How far did his corruption reach? Did it extend into his personal life? Was he cheating on Constance? Was he abusive? Did he gamble? Do drugs? Just who was Michael Murphy? He was certainly more interesting than I had gathered in my preliminary investigation.

Back in the front room, I pulled up to the bar to wait for Connie. This wasn't the best place to meet a woman for the first time. A bit loud. A bit boisterous. I had wanted to look around, get a feel for Murphy. I was glad I had. He was shady. Did Constance know? Was she involved? How did Veronica figure into this? I ordered Roses and rocks, sipped it, and scanned the mirror behind the bar for the flash of blonde hair. I felt out of place with my greying hair, sports coat, and U of K cap among kids wearing end of season shorts, sandals, ironic tee shirts, and sincere U of L caps. We would leave. I'd take Connie somewhere else, but first she had to arrive. It was quarter after, and I hadn't heard from her. I finished my drink, ordered another, and my phone rang. It was Connie. Nasal voice. Sharp diction. She was east end. She was caught in traffic on the Watterson Expressway. I suggested a change of plans. Could she meet me at the Big Four Bridge? We'd walk across the river to Jeffersonville. Have a quiet dinner in one of the small places there. She said she would call the agency to let them know about the change of plans. She'd call me when she got in the parking lot.

My drink arrived. I tipped the glass back to finish the bourbon then slid it back across the bar. Leaving two fives, I turned for the door.

13

I'd never used an escort before. Never even been on a blind date. I gripped the wheel hard, as I turned left across from Cave Hill Cemetery and drove down East Broadway toward downtown. Passing through the tree-lined section of Victorian houses, I thought of Francesca. She had loved Victorians. We had talked about getting one of the big three-story jobs in Old Louisville before we bought the brick square in Pleasure Ridge. Just didn't have the time or money to fix one up. I reached the end of the tree canopy and entered a more urban, commercial environment on the outskirts of downtown proper. Low, modern buildings with small trees and shrubs lined both sides of Broadway. Down the street, I saw a train overpass and, beyond that, the tall buildings of downtown. There was only a small area I considered "city." An area with densely-packed tall buildings and no intended signs of nature. It was maybe twenty-five blocks. I continued on East Broadway through the hodgepodge of old and new, turned right on Second Street, and headed toward the river. There was more traffic here, closer to the city center.

In my youth, downtown was dead after business hours, but now it was an entertainment destination. There was Riverfront Park, Whiskey Row, and Fourth Street Live. Little remained of the seedy peep shows and strip clubs that were once so prevalent. Just before entering the Second Street Bridge, I veered right to go down the hill and under it. This part of town reminded me of parts of Chicago where the L goes over the streets, but Louisville is just an overgrown southern town complete with a Confederate monument, squarely facing the much larger Union monument to the north in Indianapolis. I tooled along beneath the steel beams until I reached Witherspoon and turned right. It was getting near sunset, and I hoped to meet Connie before dark so I could get a good look at her.

To my left, the Great Lawn stretched out to the river. Lots of people were enjoying the last of the day playing soccer and tossing balls. At the baseball stadium, I turned left onto East River Road and soon turned into the parking lot at the base of the Big Four Bridge. The city had converted that old train bridge to pedestrian use a few years before, and walking across it into Indiana was a popular activity with locals and visitors alike.

I walked to the base of the ramp and stood. The sun neared the horizon, and the air was much cooler here next to the river. I took a deep breath and let it out all at once. My body relaxed, and I let my thoughts unwind and flow.

Downstream, The I65 Bridge stood half finished. The piers were in place and the deck was just coming together. Large crane booms reached high above the whole thing and into the sunset sky. I looked at the barges moored alongside the piers and recalled the Fourth of July deaths.

The city had put on its annual fireworks show, and, as usual, a large crowd had gathered to watch. Most were on the Great Lawn. Others watched from the Indiana side, and some with the means and opportunity watched from pleasure crafts on the river. It had been raining off and on for a couple weeks, and the river flowed high and fast. At some point during or after the show, a pontoon boat with its merrymaking occupants drifted into a barge and capsized. A few people were rescued, but three were not. Days later, their bodies were recovered. I thought it was interesting that the man, who I assumed was the largest of the three, was found hung up on the Falls of the Ohio, while the woman, who I assumed was lighter, made it over the falls to be found much farther downstream. The child, being the smallest, drifted for many miles in the river as it curved past Portland, the west end, Shively and Pleasure Ridge to finally be spotted and recovered near the Mill Creek power plant in Valley Station.

When I played by the river at the old Greenwood boat dock as a youngster I thought I would see a body floating by or on shore. It seemed ·such a common occurrence, but truly it was not. It was just so archetypal and symbolically fitting that the river should be a mode of transport for the dead that once the notion had entered my mind it seemed inevitable that I'd see a floating corpse: bloated, discolored, skin scraped and scuffed, eyes missing.

My phone rang. I looked at the number to see it was Connie. I had forgotten about her. That is the magic of the river. It flows. The ocean surges and brings everything back. Everything in it returns ground up and transformed. But the river flows on and carries things away and it had carried my mind thirty years into the past. I cleared my throat and answered the phone. She was here. In the parking lot. Could I meet her at her car? Blue Solara. Sure. Now what was it I wanted from her? What did I hope to get out of Connie? Veronica was in trouble. At least Constance thought she was. Connie may know her. She may have information about her or her situation. I had to stay focused. Man, I wanted a drink. Something to hold in my hand and sip. Something strong. I had to gain her trust and convince her I meant Veronica no harm. If I knew more about Veronica I could pretend to be her brother or some long-lost relative. No. I'd have to play it straight. I'm a private detective. I'd been hired by a concerned party to locate Veronica. This conversation could happen in the parking lot, but a nice walk over the river with a view of the setting sun might soften her up. Women are like that. You have to dial in their mood before making the proposition.

14

The blue Solara's smooth lines stood out against the more square vehicles in the parking lot. I walked toward it and saw her inside. She looked in the rearview and applied lipstick. I waited on the sidewalk in front of the car. When she had finished putting on the lipstick she looked through the windshield and I saw her face. Very nice. Roundish and smooth. Platinum blonde hair cut short. Just below her ears. I nodded, and she smiled slightly. She put her lipstick away then continued doing something in her lap as though she hadn't seen me. What was she doing? Was she putting a piece in her purse? That would have been a good idea. Not necessary in this instance but a good precaution to take in her line of work. I felt awkward standing in front of her car and watching her as though she were a movie projected onto the windshield. I turned away for a moment. Swallowed a couple pills. When I looked back, she was still fiddling about. What was she doing? After another minute, I caught her eye and made a gentle beckoning gesture with my fingers. She smiled and closed her eyes for a moment. When she opened them she was looking to her left. Then it hit me. She wanted me to open her door. Well, of course. She was a lady, and I was to play the proper gentleman. I could do that.

I walked to the door and after another brief moment, just a hiccup, she pressed the button to unlock the door. I opened it, and she stepped out and tilted her head back to look me in the eyes. She was beautifully small, and her eyes were ice blue almost light grey. She held out her delicate hand for me to take.

"Jimmie Star."

"Pleased to meet you. I'm Connie."

"Care to walk across the bridge?"

She smiled and said, "If you like, but let's sit and talk first."

I led the way between cars. Her hand was light in mine, not tugging or jolting as we stepped up onto the sidewalk, and I was careful not to jerk it. In just the few minutes of our acquaintance, she had reversed the roles. Though I was the paying customer, she was in charge. She was the center of attention, and I was her escort.

We took our time walking to a bench overlooking the river. I had to take smallish steps to avoid dragging her. That made me feel like I was accompanying some state dignitary or religious leader on a public procession. All my attention focused on her. Not jostling her. When we reached the bench, she sat first and patted the seat for me to join her. She looked at me and smiled, and I blushed like a bashful boy.

"Lovely weather we're having."

She wanted to talk about the weather. Getting to know you chit chat. Not easy. Directness is my strength. Directness and deception. This was something new. I had to draw it out a bit. Show more in style than substance.

"I love this time of year. The sun is warm, but the air is crisp and cool."

"Me too. Very nice." She smiled. "I especially like the leaves turning. Little by little, we get a whole new environment to live in."

I wanted to cut the chit chat and get straight to the questions, but that would never work, so I sat quietly for a moment and watched as people of all sorts walked by. There were sporty people walking fast, slobs with pant bottoms dragging, frazzled moms with their nagging kids, a few singles but mostly couples young and old. Connie sat poised beside me. She was a lady, and to anyone walking by we were a couple. She gazed at me, and I struggled to recall the topic. "The leaves are nice. Brown and yellow and red."

She looked at me sternly. "Why did you call the agency?"

"What do you mean?"

She licked her lips. "I mean why did you need a companion for this evening?"

I shifted my eyes to the river. Its rippling surface sparkled with red and pink light from the setting sun, and I thought of Manet paintings.

"Do you like Impressionism?"

She studied me. "So you could talk art appreciation?" She turned her head slightly but kept her eyes on me. "If you like, but I'm curious." She shifted her eyes away then back. "Most people that hire an escort have an event to attend or they're looking for a particular type of woman. Maybe a looker or a lady like

66

myself. Perhaps I'm not the type you were looking for?"

"No, you're perfect. It's just. I need some information."

"Are you police?"

"No. Private detective."

"Jimmie Star. Of course." She stroked my hand gently. "I'm so sorry."

I turned away and drew a deep breath. "I'm looking for a girl." I gazed into her eyes. "You may know her. Name's Veronica Rene." I saw the spark of recognition in her eyes, felt her keen attention and concern. "She may be in danger."

"What kind of danger?"

"Not sure." I took a breath. "When's the last time you saw her?"

"Well, we aren't friends, but I know her when I see her." She nodded. "It's not like we work in the same office. We're more like private contractors. But I can spot a lady for hire, especially one that so much favors Veronica Lake, you know, the forties actress. The one with the Peekaboo hair."

"Peekaboo hair?"

"It hung down to cover one eye." Now that I think about it. The Palace Theatre is showing one of her movies tomorrow night. If she's a fan, you may find her there."

"Okay. Thank you." I stood up to leave, and she cleared her throat. When I looked at her, she held out her hand.

15

After walking Connie to her car, I headed back to Berry Boulevard. It was still early, and I had a sweet tooth. Candy filled my thoughts. Sweet Candy wrapped in cellophane. Perhaps I'd see the movie tomorrow. I really doubted I'd find Veronica there. Still, it might be a useful fieldtrip. That was tomorrow. Tonight I had other plans, and they involved something sweet crossing my lips, something luscious on my tongue. I hoped I wasn't jumping the gun. Maybe she didn't want what I wanted. And what was that? What did I want with Candy? I wanted to forget. I wanted sweet oblivion. I wanted to be washed clean of the past, the haunting memory of that night on the sidewalk when I held my dying wife. She would always be with me. She had had her effect, and I would never truly forget her. Her smile. The way it made me feel. But it was time to move on. Or was I kidding myself? Was I chasing some ephemeral joy, clinging to some flimsy bit of driftwood in an effort to stay afloat in the flood of pain and grief and despair that engulfed me? I poured myself a bourbon with ice and studied the way the ice reflected and refracted the flickering fluorescent light. There was no difference between suicide and dying from drink and debauchery. Both trips lead to the worms. At least with Candy I'd have a sweet taste on my lips when the Hell mouth opened to swallow my miserable corpse.

I stumbled next door to the Fog Light. Peaches saw me walk in and approached. She said Candy was gone for the night and I should try again tomorrow. I half smiled and thanked her. She hugged me, and I felt her ribs just beneath her skimpy top and taut skin, and shivers travelled my spine. I pressed against her, felt her bones and tendons and dry hair, and something in me grew heavy. My soul or spirit or whatever. Something sank deep and kept sinking, spiraling down.

16

I'd grown accustomed to waking on my couch with no idea how I'd gotten there. Nothing I could do about it except rub a hand across my eyes and struggle to sit up. My head felt warped and compressed to the point of exploding, and a whining tone pierced my mind like an emergency alarm filling a night sky that roiled with clouds and lightning. My heart ached with the familiar pain. The frigid pain. I took a few of the Oxi and looked for my bottle, but truthfully, at this point, any bottle belonging to anyone or laying in any gutter would have done the trick. When I found it, I took a hurried gulp, then someone knocked at my front door. Candy. Or should I have called her Mary? She had told me her true name, but I still thought of her as Candy. Just more real and fragile. When she saw me looking, she gestured for me to unlock the door, which I did. She pushed it open and threw herself on me in a great embrace. She had heard what happened. I'd passed out. Peaches and the bouncer carried me in the back door of my office. Her face was animated with care and concern, and her eyes glistened with tears.

She had been out all night. I didn't ask for details but imagined fast cars and drugs and Mary howling at the moon. I figured she could use some coffee, so I excused myself to make a pot. After adding the filter, grounds, and water, I realized she had gone to the back room. I walked there and found her on my couch, head bowed and left arm extended. She held a syringe in her hand. Another syringe sat by her side. I watched her push the plunger in with her thumb, then she looked up at me, struggled to meet my gaze. She was gone. Like the Zen mantra: Gone. Gone. Gone. I wanted to experience that peace, but mostly I wanted to experience the suffering of its absence. A wail built in my soul. It was the mournful, anguished, lamenting expression of despair, clawing at the core of my being. It was the sound of Munch's screamer, issuing forth from the all-encompassing pit of naked anxiety I had gazed into in the Gagel apartment. It had gazed back. It had sucked me into its trance, hypnotized me with the cooing of doves. Now they called to me again, lured me like a siren bent on seeing me dashed upon the stones of my suffering. Doc Laraunt had stepped from the inky darkness to kill my wife. He had killed her to make me suffer longing and despair, but there was more. There was guilt and shame. I could have prevented it. I could have backed down when Laraunt sent his man to beat me, but I'd been too stubborn, too full of piss and vinegar. Guilt was crushing me. It was too much guilt. More than I deserved for my stubbornness. There was something more to the story. Something I'd forgotten. Repressed. I needed to pay penance for this dark and unknown deed. Is this what Mary had offered back at the park? She had held something. Was it this? The suffering of desperate addiction?

Would I gain absolution by bowing to this horrible god? My eyes turned to the sharp point of the needle, where a drop of the clear drug glistened in dim light. I imagined pain and anguish there, compressed like light in a black hole, as I studied the veins of my arm and picked one I hoped would go straight to my heart. I pierced it and pulled the plunger back a little to see a swirl of blood rush into the plastic tube where it mixed into the liquid heroin. I slowly pressed the plunger, and warmth radiated through my arm and into my heart, then throughout my body in a wave of bliss, flowing over my suffering form like flood water slowly rising to submerge a stone statue of Hercules. My tense muscles softened, and my joints loosened. All pain subsided, and the jabbering ship of thought sank beneath soothing waters of sensation. My awareness swam in the mellow warmth, and I looked at Mary, curled small by my side. As I began to nod off, I looked into her eyes. They were dark and compelling, her gaze unchanging. I sank into it, fell into the trance of the sameness of her gaze, and her love travelled to me across webs of entanglement. Waves of compassion undulated from her to enter my body at the solar plexus. Tingling flowed through me, as her yellow love mixed with my red agony. Her love flowed through me and encompassed me, and I dwelled in it like a bird in the sky, and I began to transform and heal. Then, Francesca's face rose in the strange sky of my imagination. It was horrible.

Dark grey and leathery. Her eyes, wide and furious, stared down on me, as thunder rolled, and my heart filled with guilt and shame. My body quaked, but I didn't wake from the dream. Tears seeped onto my eyelids and trickled down my cheeks. Francesca claimed my soul. She was its master, and she would punish me for what I'd done.

17

The Palace was an old movie theater on Fourth Street. Built in 1928, it had astounded concert and moviegoers since then with its ornate interior and intricately carved busts of famous artists and thinkers which adorned the arched ceiling of the lobby. I was there to see a Noir classic, "The Blue Dahlia," featuring Veronica Lake. I hoped to find the missing Veronica Rene there. Judging by her wavy blond hair and alias, she had some interest in the actress. I hoped her interest would draw her to the theatre that night. Perhaps I'd solve the case and still have time to see Mary. The movie was already showing when I arrived, so I sat in the balcony beneath the sky-blue expanse of arched ceiling and scanned the audience for the glint and flash of bright blond hair. No luck. I turned my attention to the screen.

It took me a few minutes, but I figured out the plot. Alan Ladd's character had returned from World War II to find his wife living it up with another man. While he was away, his son had died, and, as the plot thickened, his wife confessed she was responsible for his death. She was killed, and Ladd, the chief suspect in her murder, went on the run. Then Veronica Lake drove into Ladd's life. She was a natural beauty. Symmetrical face. Plump lips. Wavy blonde hair. She and Ladd flirted for a bit then, in what seemed to be an important scene, he announced his intention to abandon her. She wanted to know why, and he said, "Every man has seen you. Somewhere. The trick is to find you." I remember that line distinctly because it didn't make sense within the context of the movie. It didn't relate to the plot or the characters' relationships or even the events of the moment. It didn't make sense except as a ham-handed attempt to infuse the tale with a Jungian theme. As I pondered the line, a petite blonde stood from an orchestra seat. Her wavy hair obscured her right eye, and my heart fluttered. It was her. It was Veronica Rene.

I stood and watched her adjust her coat. Then she entered the aisle and walked slowly up the incline. I should have gone straight for the stairs when I saw her but stood like an awestruck boy as she moved with subtlety and grace to the back of the theatre. When she disappeared beneath the balcony, a jolt passed through my body. I had to move.

I headed for the aisle but kept tripping over knees and purses. I finally made it to the balcony stairs and looked toward the entrance to see her small form pass through onto the street. My hand slid along the banister as I rushed down the stairs toward the lobby. When I reached it, my heart pounded like a sledgehammer driving stakes in my chest. I had to stop. I had to breathe. Leaning on the banister, I waited for my heartbeat and breathing to settle. When they did, I wiped the sweat from my forehead and walked toward the exit. I made it to the door, and just as I stepped from the vestibule onto the brick sidewalk, I saw her pass by in a large black 1940s convertible. I strained my eyes to get the plate. I'd have a friend on the force run it in the morning. That would lead somewhere. Or nowhere. At least I'd seen her. She looked safe and secure, but looks can deceive.

18

I was beginning to feel a bit hairy inside, kinda itchy. I'd taken the last of my Oxi back at the theatre and didn't have a script to fill. I wasn't above buying it off the street when the pain in my chest grew too intense, but at the moment it was tolerable. Just a gnawing ache that radiated strange visions of Francesca.

She was always there. Whether I knew it or not, she was there. Angry. Vengeful. I'd done her wrong. Somehow. I'd been pursuing justice. The mayor was twisted up with Laraunt. They were entangled like breeding snakes. I'd stumbled across their cabal while looking for another girl gone missing. Things happen like that in this line of work. Another man might have worked them for a payoff. Not me. Not Jimmie God Damned Star. Cock-sure and self-righteous, I rushed headlong into their nest.

The whole thing revolved around basketball and sex. Laraunt had been providing women to the university's basketball program, which used them to lure recruits. There had been some complaints about improper girls and behavior, but campus police had turned a blind eye. When things shook out, the mayor was implicated in the cover up. He had pressured campus cops to look the other way. I had the goods on him. E-mails. Personal letters. Pictures of him with some of the girls at an official function. Echoes of Monica Lewinski. I went to the chief of police. He was a good man.

The mayor made a deal. He'd step down to avoid charges. For my role in the investigation, the deputy mayor gave me the key to the city. I was set to testify against Laraunt, but that never happened. He killed Francesca and damn near killed me. I clammed up. Had I turned yellow? Had I lost the fire for justice? I don't know. Maybe. All I know is I wish it had been me instead of her. It was incredibly cruel, what he did. Marred and scarred me, but there is only one way in this life. Forward. There is no going back. One can only move forward.

It was still early, so I called Mary to see if we could get together. She was off work. I asked where she was and found her answer a bit evasive but didn't want to think about it. I wanted to see her. I wanted to lie with her and drift away in the fog of a heroine nod. Maybe this time Francesca would forgive me. I still wasn't sure what I'd done, but it would come to me in time. I asked Mary if we could meet. She said yes. She was in the Highlands. Twig and Leaf had reopened that day. Could I meet her there?

I parked on Douglass and walked in the rain to Bardstown Road. It was on the corner, a green building that stood out as an old-fashioned diner should. The place was under new management, and I could tell. When I walked in, I wasn't overwhelmed by the once-familiar pine scent of the cleaner the previous owners had used in abundance. The new owner introduced himself. Seemed like a nice guy. I didn't quite catch his name. Something Pakistani. He told me to sit anywhere, so I chose a booth by one of the large windows along Bardstown Road. I thought of taking off my rain-wet jacket but didn't want to alarm the other patrons with my pistol in its shoulder holster.

I studied the freshly-laminated menu for a moment then ordered two house salads, vegetable soups, and grilled cheese sandwiches. I turned my attention to a young couple talking about their day. Their demanding bosses and traffic and whatnot. Just telling stories. Their stories. Their day to day stories that had, to be honest, very little at stake other than their pride. I wondered if they had any notion of the suffering they might endure in this topsy-turvy world. The pain of loss. The torment of guilt. The longing for death.

The waiter spread the food across the faux granite table top. I looked at it. Everything looked good. The grilled cheese was nicely toasted, and the salad looked fresh, moist, and crisp. The soup was red and chunky with corn and peas and green beans. I heard the door open and looked up to see Mary. She was stunning. Black high-heel boots that rose up her calves to her knees. Tight blue jeans. A black and white argyle sweater that hugged the curves of her breasts. She wore a wig of black hair, piled high on her head in a nod to the old-fashioned beehive. She looked at me and smiled with the sultry allure of Amy Winehouse. Perhaps we could make love tonight. I'd heard about the effects of opiate use on libido. Heard it would kill my sex drive or ability. Oxi hadn't done it, but I was scared we would become junk buddies rather than lovers. I looked at her again and felt the stirring of desire. Time would tell, but, for now, we were on our way. I didn't know where we were headed, but it was better to have a travelling companion than trudge on alone.

19

We smoked a joint in her car then decided to get a room. I'd forgotten my expense card, but Mary knew a cheap place, so we rode south on Bardstown Road until we passed beneath the Watterson Expressway. We were headed for the Midtown Inn, an old hotel on the corner of Goldsmith Lane and Bardstown. When we got near it, a stoplight caught us, and we saw that the place had been demolished. We looked out at the piles of concrete and bricks and steel beams glowing in the last rays of the day. The scene reminded me of 9 / 11, and I fell to imagining the rumbling fire and screams and the jumpers: falling and falling. The newspaper photo had frozen their descents, but there was only one way for them to go. There was only one possible outcome. I'd closed the paper when I saw that photo. I'd closed it and hidden it away inside a box. Unable to either throw it out completely or deal with it emotionally. I still had it in a box of stuff in my office.

The car behind me honked, and I snapped out of it. I'd always been prone to such fugue state imaginings. Lately they'd been coming more and more.

As the sun settled on the horizon and grey clouds hung in the darkening sky, we continued to the next block then pulled off Bardstown to drive behind the McDonald's to the Econo Inn, known locally as the "hooker hotel." It was ground zero for drugs and prostitution in this area, and concerned citizens were constantly trying to shut it down, but the owner skimmed enough money from the illicit trade to pay off officials and remain open. The owner, it should come as no surprise, was Doc Laraunt.

It stood off the road a good piece, a poorly-lit, C-shaped grouping of two and three-story brick buildings painted an unsettling yellow brownish color with hunter green doors and railings. A faded yellow awning above the office advertised Jacuzzi rooms for 40 dollars per day or 140 per week. A few fellas wearing caps with straight bills and listening to hip hop stood on the dim porch outside a door while on the other side of the lot, a grimy guy holding a rolled newspaper walked up to the passenger side of a car. The man inside flashed a wad of cash and leaned over to talk to him through the window. Everything here was seedy, crooked, and dangerous, but it would have to do. We weren't on vacation. We wanted a place to shoot up. No view required, so even one of the rooms with plywood over the windows would have been fine. If the fire marshal was okay with it, I was too. I looked at Mary. Her eyes were dark with heavy black eyeliner. She smiled slightly. I wasn't sure what her small smile expressed. Was it compassion for me? Genuine happiness? Desperation and resignation? I couldn't read her at the moment. I'd try again when we were properly loaded. I parked in front of the office and gripped her knee. We'd stay here for a while and shoot ourselves to Palookaville. Then I'd treat her to a night in the Hyatt at Constance Murphy's expense. One of the photos of Veronica had been taken there. Perhaps someone would remember her.

I stepped from the car and walked toward the office. Beneath the tacky yellow awning stood a tall, four-tier, brown and blue, concrete fountain. I walked to it, stood before it, and watched the water cascade from the scalloped basins with a monotonous splashing that lulled me into a trance.

The water flowed and splashed, and I perceived that the fountain was the source of an inexhaustible energy from some darker spiritual dimension. This was the place where it burst forth into this realm of mundane existence. This was the Axis Mundi. The new center of my world. I looked at it and felt its energy flow through my body in a rising, bubbling torrent of desperation and depravity.

A shiver woke me, and I looked across my shoulder to Mary. She half smiled. I could barely see her through the dusty windshield. I thought she smiled.

20

The room was dank. Stale. Stanky. The bathroom a foul abode of germs. The bed was a squeaky, rundown, infested tomb covered with a raggedy polyester monstrosity nothing short of abysmal. We dared not sit on it. Instead, we sat on the floor in the corner and sought refuge in the needle. It was gloriously smooth: the molten chocolate bliss flowing through my veins like the blood of angels. I sank into luxury like a feather drifting through the blue sky to enter a cloud. All was golden eternity and lace trimmed with spider webs. She reached out to me. Stroked my arm, and a cascade of delicious sensations flowed through me, traveled every fiber of my nervous system. I had seen it once. The nervous system apart from the rest of the body. In an exhibit of bodies from China. The fibers splayed out like the strings on a glorious harp that reverberated with every touch. She played me, and my body sang the song she played. It was a celebration of life and love so moving and vital that I felt myself grow aroused beyond all normal bounds of desire. I was arousal. I was desire in the flesh. I was flesh made holy and eternal. Each stroke of her hand sent new thrills through my spine, as she coaxed new sounds from me, moaning on the floor and writhing with mounting satisfaction.

She was a masterful musician, but as her song rose to its crescendo, there came creeping into the melody the strained tones of discord and cacophony. Sevenths and ninths, jagged and stringent, hacksawed my bones as Francesca's voice, slick with Swiss accent, rose slowly to declare her charge in long wavering tones. "Youuuu killllllled meeeee."

21

I woke with a start. What had Francesca meant? I'd killed her? I felt something move along my leg. Looking down, I saw bedbugs crawl across my skin. They skittered along my bare legs, inside my boxers, and beneath my tee shirt. I wriggled in disgust. Wanting to jump up, I barely struggled to my knees to kneel over Mary, who lay still, half naked and rife with the large, amber-colored, ancient-looking beasts. One crawled across her pale cheek. Another crept along the contour of her exposed breast. I felt a bite on my chest and smacked at the bug to trap it against my sternum. Then I pressed its plump body beneath my fingertip. It expired in an explosion of blood, which seeped through my tee shirt. Waves of disgust flowed through me. I felt gross as though I'd been dipped in putrid piss and scuzzy stuff from the back of the fridge. I had to shower. Had to purify myself of their taint. I didn't want to leave Mary at their mercy, so I shook her shoulder. Her body rocked loosely with my movements. She didn't respond. I shook her more forcefully, tried to rattle her bones a bit. Stillness and silence. Icy black fingers tore through my sandy form, and I became tingling and shivers. I looked left and right then back to her. Was she dead? I checked her neck for a pulse. Nothing but flesh, cold and clammy. I recoiled and gasped.

As quickly as I could manage, I gathered my things and wiped down the room. Anything I had touched. Then I parted the dusty curtains to see darkness and rainy reflections of neon. I should have called an ambulance. Maybe the police, but that would have ended my career. Consorting with drug users. Using. They'd have pulled my license for sure.

I turned back to see Mary, a crumpled heap of cold flesh, crawling with bugs, and a rush of chills ran through my body. I stared at her, and gradually my fear and disgust turned to acceptance.

I went to her, knelt beside her, and looked at her face, small and lovely. Her head was tilted slightly, and her purple hair radiated around it like rays from some dark star that may exist in a far distant part of the universe. Her cheeks hung loosely. Her lips were parted. She looked peaceful and calm. My body radiated warmth and compassion, and I felt it happen. My heart sent out its feelers, its lines of communication. We had mingled before, but this was different. Stronger. More intense. My heart swelled with the warmth and light of love, and I extended my hands toward her. My body vibrated with an unusual energy. I had experienced it only once before. On my wedding day. The dank room came alive with clarity, and I felt the energy travel down my arms and radiate from my fingertips. I found her there. Something. A slight glow of life. Tears formed on my eyelids, as I poured myself into the effort. Every bit of free energy,

I sent to her across the lines of entanglement. We became one, body and soul bound ineffably by love, and the life in her stirred. Her eyes fluttered, and I collapsed on her in a torrent of tears.

22

It took Mary a few minutes to process her experience and gather her thoughts. Once she'd gotten herself straight, she told me about a dazzling white light. "It was beautiful," she said, "but terrifying. I don't know how anything could be so enticing and terrible at the same time, but it was, and I felt myself repelled by it, turned away, and rejected. Then I drifted through a rainbow of lights. Red and yellow and blue. All the while, I grew colder and my mind fell away until it was nearly gone. It wasn't bad. Dying. No pain or fear remained as I drifted for what seemed like forever. Then I felt you reach out for me, and all at once, I longed to be with you in this world. I wanted everything it has to offer. The pain and misery and joy. All of it." She half smiled. "Then I woke up to see you." She looked into my eyes. "How can I ever thank you?"

I led her to the bathroom, sat her on the toilet seat, and undressed myself. Then I started the water so it would heat up. I peeled off her loose top and satin panties and looked at her standing naked before me. She was gorgeous, perfectly curvy, and small like a statuette.

We stepped into the shower. The steaming water beat down on her pale flesh and turned it bright red with warmth. I pressed myself against her, felt her bottom against my thighs. Holding her from behind, I slid my hands up to cup her breasts. I kneaded them firmly, felt her nipples stiffen. Oh how I wanted to make love to her, but not here. This place was out of the question. We'd get a room at the Hyatt. So what if she was supposed to work? She was my girl now. Laraunt had plenty to choose from.

We didn't want to dress in our infested clothes but had no other choice within the bounds of reason, so we shook them out in the bathroom and watched the tiny beasts crawl in high contrast against the white porcelain. After doing our best to rid our clothes of bedbugs, we put them on, cringing the whole time. We couldn't wait to get out of them, so we headed straight for her car.

***

She pulled up behind my truck, and we held hands for a while in the dead of night. I wished the sun would rise, longed to see the black sky lighten. I felt her warmth radiate to me and wanted to say something to express how close I felt to her, but no words came. I just caressed her hand and, after a sigh, leaned over to kiss her. She wrapped me in her arms, and I melted into her embrace. Mentally. Physically. Emotionally. She had nearly died. Somehow, I'd brought her back. Had the drugs made it possible? People can do strange and wonderful things when they are under stress. A hundred pound woman can pick up a car when her child is stuck under it. Stuff like that. But I had brought Mary back from the edge of death. That's strong stuff.

I looked at her, smiled, and stroked her cheek.

"I'll stop using." She patted my hand. "I promise."

It was a promise she would never keep.

23

I stripped at the door, threw my clothes outside on the crumbling asphalt, then, after a brief search for bugs, walked to the back room of my office to collapse on the worn leather couch. The evening had been too much. I needed to recover. A few hours of sleep would do the trick, but no matter what I tried, sleep would not come. Itching and twitching from opiate withdrawal, I tossed about for a while. Francesca came flitting on the edges of my consciousness, in the dark corners of my psyche. She glowed a dull green in her wedding dress, and her hair continually waved about as though moved by a steady breeze. She stood completely still except to raise a hand and repeat her accusation that I'd killed her. When she did, my heartbeat turned spastic with fear and bewilderment, and the familiar pain swelled. Sitting on the edge of the couch, I put a hand to my chest. I wanted to locate the pain, hold it in my hand, and turn it around to study it. Perhaps I could take a knife and dig out the slug. But that wouldn't change a thing. That bullet didn't cause my pain. She did. I knew that. I felt the ache but knew it wasn't true, physical pain. It was the torment of guilt and longing and the trigger of my addictions. I still didn't know what I'd done. I hadn't killed her like she claimed, but ghosts don't listen to reason. They feel.

I had the day to do as I pleased. What would that be? Bottles and pills? No more. I'd experienced something different when I saved Mary. Sweet love energy. I'd felt it flow through me. I had a second chance, a fresh opportunity with Mary. I'd need to woo her away from her lifestyle with a better option. But I was a lowlife too. A washed up hero. Drunk and stoned half the time. I needed to change, and I'd start today. Lay off the pills and heroine. That stuff was beginning to take hold of me. It seemed the moment I pulled the needle from my arm in the Econo Inn I was ready to melt down another dose. No more. Getting clean would be hard, but I'd do it for Mary. Besides, the first symptoms of withdrawal had already set in. The train had left the station with me aboard.

I'd felt increasingly irritable and nervous that morning, while I made a few phone calls. It started with John Harper, a friend on the police force. While punching in the tag number from the black convertible he talked, but I didn't really make conversation. There was a slight hum on the line, and I couldn't help but focus on it. I heard his voice, but the combination of his throaty growl and the hissing static really set my nerves on edge.

"Registered to Doc Laraunt." His car wreck of a voice mingled with the phone hum to make my arms tingle, so I hurried off the phone.

It didn't surprise me that the convertible was Laraunt's, but why was she driving it? Seemed he was taking good care of her. Still, judging by her departure in the middle of the movie, she must have been at his beck and call. Perhaps he'd messaged. Maybe he needed her to meet a last-minute client. Someone important. Anything was possible, but two things were certain. I'd seen her, and she was driving his car. I'd barely caught a glimpse, but it was her. Whoever she was, she was his.

I thought of a frontal approach to Laraunt, and fear immediately rose in me. I'd freaked out in Paoli. Ran at the mention of his name, so I certainly wasn't ready to face him. He'd hurt me bad, and I was scared. Besides, Veronica didn't seem to be in great peril. She wasn't turning tricks in a fleabag motel as I'd feared.

I'd check out the Hyatt. See what turned up. Mary and I would have dinner, drinks, and a room courtesy of Constance Murphy. We'd get ourselves all fat and happy then make love.

I called Constance. She was pleased I'd spotted Veronica Rene alive and well. Said she wanted pictures. I squeezed the phone in my hand. That damned hiss was cutting through me, making me itch and twitch. Hoping to conceal my nervousness and irritability, I took a deep breath and told her I'd get back to her when I had the pictures and more information.

I was sweating by the time I dialed up Mary. My body was really churning with pain, but I kept myself together long enough to ask her to prepare for a special evening. Put on her nicest dress. Do herself up. She was nervous about ditching work. Didn't want to upset her manager at the Fog Light. I tried to remain patient as I asked her to quit that place. She said she would think about it.

"Fair enough."

By noon the pain spread through me, made me pace about my office like a caged bear. I swayed and twitched and turned my gaze this way and that, until my restlessness and frustration gave rise to the desire to flay the skin from my arms. I wanted to rip it off, shred it with my fingernails, and plaster the concrete walls with it. I threw my head back in exasperation as my constricted heart pumped out a syncopated rhythm. It seemed every cell of my body had become a hungry mouth to feed. Baby birds in the nest of my flesh begging for the narcotic sludge. And when I didn't provide the hit, those vicious, selfish, unconscious cells threw a tantrum like any toddler would. It seemed they held their breath, and a strange sense of suffocation set in. It was as though I were under water, compressed from all sides and unable to breathe or move freely. I gasped for air and heard the wheezing of my lungs, as my chest quivered with effort. I thought I would die there in my office. On Berry Boulevard of all places. I slumped on the old leather couch and sweated like a cheap hooker on the vinyl seat of an old Buick. I lay there and shivered and sweated, as a ringing tone like a looped scream rang through my body and my bones vibrated and disintegrated. Pure anguish coursed through me, and Francesca assaulted my mind with her unreal presence and real absence. Just when I thought it could get no worse, I shit myself. All afternoon I wallowed in shit-smeared agony. A crying, drooling, stinking mess on the old leather couch.

Gradually, I returned to something like normal. The worst was over. I was lucky. It could have been so much worse. I'd just gotten my feet wet with hard drugs but instinctively knew what lay ahead. I would've settled down to the bottom of a dark sea of addiction never to return. Mary had led me this far, and I'd willingly followed. But I had turned back. Now she was alone in her addiction, and I'd love her no matter what she did.

* * *

I cleaned up and started to dress. While I was looking through my clothes, a funny thing happened. Nothing from the pile of clothes that I normally wore seemed appropriate. Nothing was quite good enough for the day ahead. I opened a box of nicer clothes. Things I hadn't worn since Francesca's death. Sport coats and ties I used to wear when we went out. Back of the closet stuff. Then I found it, folded neatly inside a plastic bag. My wedding suit. The same suit I'd worn to her burial. It was dark grey. Solid. Made from smooth, soft wool. I found the shirt too. White. Glistening white. Crisply folded collar.

The tie was there. Black with faint burgundy swirls. I laid the suit on the couch to look at it, and my mind went back to that cold winter day, nearly a year ago.

We'd gathered on the windy slope in Cave Hill Cemetery. Her parents weren't there. Couldn't make it in time. I'd called them to break the news, but they already knew. They were broken and tearful, and I felt their hatred of me. I'd promised to love and protect their daughter, but I'd failed. Her father's stern voice came across the line, across thousands of miles, to cut through me with a single question. "How did it happen?" I couldn't answer. Overwhelmed with shame, I dropped the phone and let it lay on the floor.

It was just me, the honor guard from the city, and a preacher, standing in the cold breeze and snow. I hovered beside the casket, as tears rolled down my cheeks. The preacher spoke a few words. I watched the casket slowly sink into the grave, and my heart went with it. My heart was buried with her. Six feet below the grass on that hillside. My heart, my soul, had been entombed with her. She had taken it down in the form of a secret. Since then, I'd fallen apart. I'd lost the house. Our home. I'd drank myself into a continual stupor and flirted with heroin addiction. But, with a little help, I'd reclaim my heart.

I needed help and knew just the person. A hypnotist named Fischer. He'd put me in touch with her. He'd conjure her up from the labyrinth of my mind. I got on the phone, heard the clear dial tone, and called Fischer. I explained my situation. Tormenting visions, pain, and a possible secret. He asked me to come straight over.

I drove to his office on Preston, near Eastern Parkway. It was in a converted home. Just a room set aside for his practice. He sat me in a leather recliner and asked me to make myself comfortable. I settled into the chair and let out a breath. He began to speak in a mellow voice, guiding me ever deeper into the crippling chill in my chest. Shivers ran through my arms, my teeth clenched, as I entered into the pale blue torment. Tears rose to my eyes, and I shook with grief, as Francesca revealed herself to me. She was beautiful in her wedding dress. Her bright eyes peered deep within me, and I longed for her. The pain gripped me, and I resisted it by tensing in the chair. It grew stronger. There was no use fighting. This pain would be the death of me if I didn't face it. I drew a deep breath and relaxed again into the cold chill of my memory of her.

It was our wedding day, and we stood outside the Lutheran church in Thawil, Switzerland. Bright Alpine light flowed through the open square in front, and bells rang through the town. Joy swirled through my body and mind, and I basked in the clarity of the day and communion with well-wishers. I had married my true love, and everything glowed in an exuberant display of radiance and beauty. I felt the joy of all existence. Everything glowed with it, sang with it, and our unified hearts joined in stirring song. Our one soul sang joyously along with horns and strings until the song rose to a great crescendo. But my experience was overwhelmed by comic book explosions of angular light and screeching nightmare screams, as I saw a dark figure from the corner of my eye. I turned, spinning Francesca around like a shield between us. I felt the explosion and impact. Icy water filled my soul like filthy winter slush in a roadside gutter. Sorrow swelled in my chest, and I cried. I had sacrificed her to save myself. I was guilty.

My body quivered as my heart poured out regret and sorrow in a torrent of tears. Then I felt her forgiveness flow over me like water from a sacred spring of redemption, and the pain in my chest faded away.

I swung my truck into the parking lot at Wildwood Condominiums in Buechel and called to let Mary know I had arrived. She slurred that she was ready. Come on up. I thought she could have come down. That would have saved some time, but that night I wouldn't rush. I would be a gentleman, and she would be my lady. I entered the breezeway and climbed the stairs to the second level. Her unit was at the rear, near the pool. Wondering what she would be wearing, I walked to her door and stood for a moment to feel the energy flow through my body. I was giddy as a schoolboy dancing his first slow dance with a girl. I knocked and waited. What kind of dress would it be? Would she have on the Amy Winehouse wig? I knocked again and began to worry. I'd just spoken to her. She sounded drunk, but that shouldn't have stopped her from opening the door. Had she gone for a bump? A little nudge of heroin to get her through?

I stared at the door. It was a flat slab. I saw the brushstrokes in the hunter green paint and the barest hint of my reflection. The broad outline of my dark form and lighter face. I rubbed my hands together and went to knock again. When I did, the door swung open to reveal Mary, standing in a strapless, floral print dress, which, though not tight, kissed her curves. Her hair was her own purple. A short white sweater covered her arms. She smiled a sloppy, head-tilting smile and spun around in a slow, clumsy circle to show herself. Her beauty entranced me, but it was marred by her manner. Drunk. Stoned. Whatever. She was wasted. Slurring. Stumbling. Barefoot. I stepped into her place and followed her to the couch, where she sat down all at once. Kinda threw herself onto it, and laid back. Legs spread. I could see the soft roundness of her thighs, shining in satiny white hose beneath the billowing red and yellow dress. Her head lulled sloppily to the side and her glossy mouth hung open a little. She lifted a hand in a sloppy wave toward a few liquor bottles, standing on a narrow table. "Help yourself."

I resisted the urge to look more closely. Didn't want to be tempted. Hadn't sworn off liquor but wanted to take care of her first. She would be out for a while, so I took off my suit coat and looked for a place to hang it. There was no closet in the combination living and dining room, and, other than the couch, very little furniture that deserved that name. Just a pile of sticks and cloth and padding where there once had been a chair. Picked and torn to shreds, it laid in the blank space of the corner like the rotting corpse of a beached whale on an expanse of sand. I looked at the ragged pile, and a strange shiver skittered through me. I turned to look at Mary, sprawled on the threadbare couch, and noticed a few sores on her cheek.

I went down the hall a bit and found the coat closet, which was filled to capacity with jackets and coats of all kinds, so I ventured further down the hall, past the bathroom to the bedroom. I pushed open the door to see her bed, piled high with rumpled blankets and pillows. Panties and stockings lay scattered on the carpeted floor, and the room smelled of vanilla. I opened her closet to see another vast array of clothes. Silky things and sequined things and leather things. Lots of things I'd seen her wear at the club. A week before, I'd have paid for the privilege to snoop around her place. I may even have lingered over her unconscious body to admire the curving forms or even run an appreciative hand along them. But not now. Concern had grown alongside desire, and curiosity had grown as well, so I looked for the box. Everyone has one. A box of private things. Mementos. Reminders. Symbols. I scanned the room. Bedside table. No. Dresser top. No. Top dresser drawer. Fresh panties and bras. A few dollars. A stash of Oxi and weed. I opened the baggie and sniffed the grass. Premium stuff. There was a glass pipe and lighter too. I lingered with it in my hand then thought about her in the other room. Was there something I could do? Seemed she was mainly drunk. Maybe she'd taken some pills. She'd sleep it off. I picked up the brown prescription bottle and shook it. The pills inside rattled, and I instinctively, almost defensively, threw it back into the drawer, which I closed. I opened the next one to find slinky things. Nighties and stockings, shiny and sleek. I

102

dug a bit deeper and found it. An old chocolates box. Heart-shaped. Red. I pulled it out and sat on the bed. This would tell the tale. Her hopes and dreams. Her fears and weaknesses. All would be represented in the contents, unconsciously collected.

I was about to open her heart, delve deep into her secret life, so I savored the moment. Took the time to shake the box gently and heard something substantial clunk around inside. The image of a round of ammunition flashed through my mind. Then, when I moved it side to side, I heard papers scuff and slide. Love letters perhaps. I slid a hand across the top and along the curving side until I felt the edge of the lid. Then I began to slide the top off and heard something in the other room. A low groan. I cast my eyes toward the door and froze. Perhaps she was dreaming. Perhaps her soul felt my intended invasion and offered its resistance. Regardless, I slid the lid from the box and looked inside to see a wallet-sized school portrait of Mary. She was maybe eleven. Long brunette hair. Big, toothy smile. Sweet and innocent. I took it out and set it on the bed. Next up was a Foo Fighters concert ticket. She would have been about six when Kurt died, so maybe she was a legitimate Foo fan.

Then I saw what had clunked around. It was a ring. I picked it up to see it was a senior ring from Pleasure Ridge Park High School. Class of 2005. But she hadn't graduated. She had dropped out after the rape. That's when she started to slide down the muddy slope toward her current situation.

There was a scrap of newsprint. The Courier Journal masthead with the date January, 15, 2004 and another photo. A young man. Neatly trimmed goatee and slicked back hair. The last thing in the box was a tightly folded piece of yellow paper. I opened it to find a hand-written composition.

Revenge

I seek revenge not just justice but revenge. I want him to see my face just like I remember seeing his. I want to have total control and power over him, while he lays there helpless. I want him to be haunted by this for the rest of his life. I will no longer be his victim. He will be mine!

I put everything back into the box, put the box back into the drawer, and went to her. She was my lady. I was her knight errant.

26

She slept, and I sat by her side. Darkness fell quickly, and I thought of nothing but her rapist, quivering before her. She wanted to have the power. Fair enough. That would never solve the world's problems, but who am I to judge her wishes. I was no saint. I'd learned that at Fischer's office. Francesca had let me know what a heel I'd been. I could find the guy if Mary would give me his name. I could arrange a situation. Something cozy for the three of us. Something private with me holding my Smith and Wesson and Mary smiling a bit while he whimpered and begged her forgiveness.

Stroking her cheek, I wanted to ask her the rapist's name but didn't want to tip my hand. I would find out when she was ready. She had told me about the rape, so I would find out the scumbag's name soon enough. She stirred, and I looked into her shame-filled eyes.

"I ruined our special night."

"Nonsense." I smiled. "We still have reservations. We'll eat and spend the night at the Hyatt." I stroked her cheek with my palm then went to her bathroom to find some aspirin. I pulled the side of the mirror, and it swung away from the wall to reveal the medicine cabinet, stocked full with various prescriptions. Mostly painkillers. I wanted to throw them out but respected her right to run her own life and fight her own fights when possible. I pushed the bottles around, looking for the aspirin. When I found the clear bottle, I took it out, popped the top, and poured out a few. Three would do. Those and some water would help with the hangover.

I went to her kitchen for a glass of water and saw that, aside from a few glasses on a counter top and several half-empty bottles of liquor and bags of chips, it appeared unused. Nothing in the fridge or cabinets. No dishes in the sink. In fact, there were no dishes or flatware at all. Seemed she wasn't much of a cook or homemaker. That was fine. All I needed at the time was a glass, which I found on the counter by the sink. I filled it with water and walked back to Mary, now sitting up on the edge of the couch. She took the pills and water from me with a slight smile.

"Thank you."

"We still have time. We can make the Oak Table."

"I just need to find my shoes. Maybe change my dress."

27

I hadn't been to the Oak Table since that night nearly a year ago. That time, Francesca and I had held hands. This time, Mary and I linked arms. The place hadn't changed. It still had the old wood and white cloth ambiance. The intimate space still sparkled with glass and silver, and Mary's eyes twinkled with reflections. She was lovely. She had abandoned the floral print number in favor of a classy black dress, plain except for a layer of chiffon around the bottom that shimmered in the low light. Very nice. She held my arm lightly as we followed the hostess to a small table in the corner. Along the way, I caught our reflection in one of the large half circle windows. We looked good. She was small and beautiful beside me, and I was handsome in my funeral suit.

I stood while she took her seat and got comfortable. Then I sat across from her with my back to the wall. From this seat I could easily survey the dining room behind her. There were many diners. The men had well-combed hair and the women had puffy dos and shiny jewelry that sparkled against their dark dresses. I was glad Mary had changed. Perhaps it was a sign of things to come. One could hope.

We held hands on the white tablecloth. I felt her skin, smooth and warm beneath my fingertips, and thought of the first time I'd seen her at the club about six months before. I'd lost the Fiddler's Heights house and the Bardstown Road office. I'd moved into the Berry Boulevard place and started going to the Fog Light for lunch. As I settled into my life post Francesca, I developed a crush on Candy. I knew she was playing me for tips and the occasional trip to the Crystal Palace, but that didn't matter. It was nice to have someone to talk with. Now she sat across from me at the Oak Table. We were serious. Something worthy of the expense of such a meal. It didn't matter that Constance was paying. The fact that I brought her here, where I'd had my last meal with Francesca, revealed what I felt for her. I squeezed her hand a little, and she smiled. I wanted to give her everything she wanted. Steak. Lobster. Revenge.

Soon we had our salads, neatly composed layers of crisp romaine and tender field greens topped with rich smoked blue cheese, tart strawberries, and sweet champagne grapes. Exquisite. When our main dishes arrived, I happened to look across Mary's shoulder. Shiny yellow blond hair. My heart fluttered. Was it Veronica Rene? I stared at the silky hair until the woman turned her face toward me. Not her. I returned to my meal, but my mind stayed with Veronica. What was her connection to Constance and Michael Murphy? I knew Michael was mixed up with Sal Lucca, maybe against his will, and that connected him to Doc Laraunt. I needed to dig deeper into Michael Murphy's affairs, but first I'd show the photo of Veronica around the Hyatt to see what folks had to say.

28

The hollow space of the Hyatt's lobby atrium rose above us in kaleidoscopic symmetry, and awe swelled in my soul. I felt as though we'd been transported to another place and time. Was it the future? The past? Was this still Louisville? It seemed like any place but. Mary, clinging to my arm, was my only reminder of my hometown. Her and the slug, which had stopped aching.

"Reservations?" The young man smiled.

"Star."

He tapped a few keys on his keyboard. "All set, Mr. Star. Do you have luggage?"

"No."

He handed me the keycard.

"By the way," I pulled the photo from my pocket, "do you know this woman?"

He looked at the picture and smiled. "Yeah. I recognize the hair. She's a regular. Used to be."

"A regular?"

"Yeah. Liked to stay on the higher floors. Outta the way." He raised a brow. "Entertained a lot of visitors. Men. Usually pretty quiet, but the last time I saw her." He cocked his head slightly. "You police?"

"Private detective."

He looked at Mary by my side.

"Her sister. We're trying to find the woman in the picture. She could be in danger."

He looked over his shoulder. "Last time she stayed here, she had a bit of trouble.

A dark-haired man beat her pretty bad. Ruined the carpet with all that blood. She ended up crying in the hall. The manager called the police, but she wouldn't talk."

"How long ago?"

"Not long. Maybe a month."

That news put a damper on the evening. The meal had been nice, but the thought of a bloody Veronica cowering in the hall killed my romantic mood. Lord knows I wanted to make love to Mary, but this was not the time. Besides, she was growing antsy. I'd seen her dig in her clutch for pills and figured we should get to our room before she went into slow mode, so I gave the desk clerk a few bucks, and we went to the elevator. By the time I unlocked the door to our room, Mary had slipped off her heels and stood small and delicate beside me. When I pushed it open, she stumbled barefoot toward the bed, where she sat fidgeting. I hung my suit coat in the closet and turned around as she pulled a baggie of heroin from her purse.

"Wanna shot?"

I looked at her, rubbing her fingertips nervously. A couple days ago I'd have agreed in a heartbeat, but not now. I was a new man. I just wanted to lay beneath the blankets with her. Feel her warmth. I knew she wouldn't rest until she had the drug flowing through her veins. I couldn't stop her and couldn't stand to see her suffer withdrawal. She was caught in a death spiral, and it broke my heart. For now, she was alive, and I loved her deeply.

I looked away but heard her strike the lighter to heat the spoon. Tears moistened my eyes, and my heart felt sluggish as though my blood had turned to mud. This passed when I turned to see her, reclining peacefully on the bed. I watched her eyelids settle over her eyes then joined her to snuggle up warm and cozy. I wanted to make her feel good like she'd done for me at the Econo Inn, so I pressed against her and felt her breathing slow. Soon, my breathing matched hers, and I could feel our hearts thumping together. I propped myself up with my left arm to look at her face, soft and round. Her eyes swam behind their lids, and the slightest hint of a smile animated her face as though her mouth were a shiny silk scarf moved by a gentle breeze. I looked at her lips, plump and smooth, then, placing my hand gently on her stomach, kissed her mouth. Her warm, soft lips slowly parted, and I felt the moistness of her breath. I kissed her more deeply, and she moaned quietly. Sliding my hand along the satin curves of her midsection, I marveled at her shape. I kissed her neck and felt her warmth on my cheek. Nudging my face into her hair, I settled down on her and slid my hand down to squeeze the thick flesh of her round bottom. She moaned again, and I panted with desire. I wanted to pull her dress off, but would she enjoy that? She was barely conscious and practically defenseless. That would be taking too much liberty. I had to reign myself in, resist my urges. I was her knight, her gentleman. She was my lady, and I'd treat her as such in our remaining time together.

29

Morning came, and I awoke to her laying by my side. Still and cold. Like a stone, she lay on the white sheet. No more a strand in this mad tangle of stimulus and response. No more a victim of men's desire and greed. She didn't look happy. She didn't look sad. She just look dead. Indifferent. Inanimate. Gone. Gone. Gone. Only her body remained. The body that had been the object of men's lust and violence and abuse.

I exhaled a shaky, choked sob, and tears flowed from my eyes. Burying my face in her hair, I cried. My body shook, as thoughts of her life gone astray flowed through my mind. Childhood abuse at the hands of her leering father and the rape by an acquaintance. The torment of her life and mine, which until then had been twisted up in a tight knot deep in my soul, unraveled in tears of grief. I collapsed onto her cold body, embraced her corpse, and wept. Her life had been driven by the pain of betrayal and violence, just as mine had been driven by the pain of guilt. We were bound by suffering, and I wept for both of us. Anguish rose from every fiber of my body and manifest as tears.

When the crying was over, I felt peace. Nearly. There was still one thing I had to do for Mary.

I swallowed hard, sat up, then, after wiping the tears from my eyes, stood at the side of the bed to look at her, laid out in her finest dress. At least she died while she was still beautiful. At least she died in a nice dress. At least she had known true love.

30

The house dick was a grumbling prick named Scanlin. He was a square-headed, bulky S.O.B. with a broom for a mustache. A former cop, he relished the opportunity to put the screws to me and look down on Mary.

"You know this junkie?" He rubbed his stiff mustache.

I was numb but had a mission, and this ass wouldn't distract me.

"Looks like a lady to me." I pressed my lips together.

"Judging by those holes in her arm and that used hypo on the table, she was a junkie." He made a tick with his tongue. "And she was using in my hotel."

"Her name is Mary."

"Well, it was." He smirked.

I watched the pen wriggle between his stumpy fingers as he wrote her name on an incident report.

"This ain't no flophouse."

"Have you called the police?"

He looked at me through narrow eyes. "On their way. Now. When'd you discover she was dead?"

"This morning."

"Y'all normally sleep in your clothes?"

The question took me by surprise, and heat rose into my face.

"See?" he said. "She's got her dress on. You said you found her dead this mornin'. That means she either slept in her clothes or didn't sleep at all."

"What does it matter?" I rubbed my fingers against my palms, "What does it matter to you?"

"Just doing my job."

"Your job is to fill out that form."

He looked at me hard. "Look here. I can make your life difficult. The story looks clear enough from where I'm standin'. You picked up this junkie and brought her to my hotel for a wild night, but the stuff was tainted. Fulla drain cleaner and rat poison."

My muscles burned with fury, and I sneered at him.

He licked his lips and continued. "Now. I have a few questions. Was it your stuff? Did you shoot her up? Either way, you're facing manslaughter charges. And why does she have her clothes on?"

I stood silent.

"I see." He half smiled. "Have it your way. I'll talk to the police when they arrive."

He didn't have long to wait. Just then, paramedics arrived and went to work verifying Mary was dead, and an officer walked through the door.

"What we got?" He nodded to Scanlin.

"Seems Mr. Star's special lady expired sometime last night. Got a used hypo on the table and marks on her arm. She's a junkie."

"Got it." He turned to me. "Got some I.D.?"

Without thinking, I handed him my P.I. license.

"Sam Spade, huh?" He smiled slyly. "Case of the missing dog?" He chuckled then returned to character. He copied my information onto a form, snapped my license toward me with a flick of his wrist, and looked me in the eye. "How'd you know the deceased?"

"Girlfriend." That term didn't seem good enough or strong enough for the love I felt for her.

"I see. She shoot up?"

"Yeah."

"You help?"

"No."

He bagged the needle and said as long as the prints on the needle didn't match my prints on file I should be clear.

"Don't leave town."

31

I stayed while they loaded her body onto the gurney and rolled it away. That was the last time I saw her as she was. Flawed. Damaged. Human. The undertaker put such a shine on her with movie star hair and makeup. He even returned her hair to its natural blond. Made her the very image of timeless perfection all wrapped in velvet and boxed in lacquered metal. She was a thing apart like a wedding ring in its box. A precious bit of eternal truth, and I didn't like it one bit.

I met her parents at the visitation. They were simple and stupid in their late fifties, but I could imagine her father being drunk enough and lewd enough and just plain ignorant and mean enough to abuse her. Unlucky girl. That's all I could think. She was just unlucky to have had those parents and lived in this time and place.

She was buried in the flat expanse of Resthaven Cemetery. Not an interesting or picturesque place but decent enough. It was the first week of November. Clouds hung motionless in the sky. The ground was crisp with fallen leaves, and the air was rich with the scent of freshly-dug earth. I looked at the casket and thought back to Francesca's funeral nearly a year before. She had been my one true love, yet I'd sacrificed her in an instinctive reaction to the threat of Doc Laraunt, stepping from the darkness. Now I stood at the side of Mary's grave, as the preacher rambled on about eternity. I'd stood by and let her inject the fatal dose. What kind of man was I? Was I the hero I'd thought I was? I wasn't sure anymore. Seems I had a yellow streak, but I could redeem myself. All I had to do was track down the bastard who sent her life down the dark path that led us all to this place and moment. I needed Peaches' help. I looked at her, wearing a black wool coat. It gave her emaciated form a bit of bulk and substance, but she was still a small presence, standing off to the side of the group, and I knew beneath that coat was a skeletal form not long for this Earth.

After the tears and interment, I stopped her as she walked toward her car. She didn't seem surprised when I asked her the rapist's name.

"Randall Lewis Johnson." She nodded. "Ya get that?" She spoke slowly and distinctly. "Randall Lewis Johnson."

"Got it."

"Lives in Portland."

32

Back in my office, I sat at the keyboard to research Randall Lewis Johnson. I quickly found a few possible matches based on name, age, and place of residence. I checked out photos and instantly recognized one. I'd seen a picture of him in Mary's box. Kind of a cool cat with dark hair combed back and a well-trimmed goatee. The rest was just as easy. A few more clicks and I had it all. Known associates. Addresses. Phone number. Vehicles. Criminal record, including convictions for sexual misconduct and statutory rape, which cost him a month in county. Currently, he was a free man, residing on Mowan Street. Licking my lips, I slid a hand beneath my suit coat to pull my pistol. Letting my fingers conform to its curves, I held the Smith and Wesson in my hand. I felt its explosive, destructive, vengeful power, a nice enhancement of my own anger, as my grip tightened to form a round fist. The handle pressed into my palm, and my finger found the trigger. Anger rose into my chest and flowed through my arms and face like fire climbing a tree. His name rose in my consciousness and passed my lips. "Randall Lewis Johnson." Imagining him cowering before me, I held the gun level and looked down the barrel. "I'm coming for you."

I'd do it that night. Find Johnson and kill him. But first, I wanted to stop by the Mad Hatter. Talk to Michael Murphy. The hotel desk clerk's story made clear

120

that Veronica's situation was worse than I'd thought. The beating at the hotel was probably not the first, and the violence would only get worse. All roads led to West Haden, and I was almost ready to face Laraunt but still didn't understand what I was dealing with. Was Veronica with Laraunt by her own free will? Was she strung out? Did she owe him money? I couldn't move on him until I knew the situation. And what about Sal Lucca and Michael Murphy? Sal was Laraunt's cohort, and it seemed a bit too coincidental that he would be involved with my client's husband. First rule in this business is never trust your client. I had a hunch Constance was deeply involved in Veronica's situation, and, if I could get him to talk, Michael Murphy could break this case wide open. I'd visit him. Talk face to face. Maybe go heavy on him.

33

It was late afternoon, and the Mad Hatter was dead. A few people eating pizza. One lonely drunk at the bar. I asked a waitress if I could speak with the owner and waited in a back corner. She rushed to the kitchen and quickly returned with Murphy, who walked toward me with an outstretched hand.

"Michael Murphy."

His hand was clammy. His grip shaky.

"Jimmie Star."

"What can I do for you?"

"Private detective."

He raised his brows.

"Investigating a missing person."

He chewed his cheek.

"Lovely young woman," I said and pulled a photo from my pocket. When he saw it, the blood drained from his face. He knew her. "Name's Veronica Rene."

"I — I don't understand."

"Well, Michael, your wife hired me."

His jaw muscles bulged as he clenched his teeth.

"Constance is very concerned about her."

He nodded.

"You know her?"

He shook his head quickly. Too quickly.

"Have another look. Maybe she's your wife's friend."

He licked his lips and took a sudden breath. "Could be." He blinked hard. "Maybe a college friend. I — I don't know all her friends."

"I see. Perhaps you're familiar with a fella named Sal Lucca?"

His expression hardened, and his eyes narrowed. "What's this all about?" He whispered. "Who are you really?"

"Private detective." I smiled. "Looking for a girl in danger."

He looked left and right. "You with Laraunt?"

A rush of tingles radiated from my heart, as I lied with a nod.

"Is she okay?" he asked.

I smiled.

"Please don't hurt her. I'll have the money soon."

"You do that." I patted him on the shoulder. "I'll be in touch."

***

As the sun set, I thought about the conversation and drove the twisting roads through Cherokee Park. Michael Murphy knew Veronica and owed Laraunt money. Laraunt was holding her as collateral and threatening to force her to work off Murphy's debt, but I'd seen her as free as a bird. So it seemed. Often the strongest chains are invisible. Love, abuse, and addiction create strong but nearly invisible ties. I'd go to West Haden to cut those ties and collect her. Let Murphy suffer the consequences. But first, I'd steal a car and drive it to Mowan Street. If Randall "the rapist" Johnson answered the door, I'd put one through his skull.

34

Mowan Street, rain-slick, moonlit, and runway straight, cut through the shotgun houses of Portland. Riding down it in the stolen Accord, I heard my tires on the wet pavement and noticed the smell of river muck. It made my skin itch. I wanted to get this thing done and get the hell outta there. Approaching the house, I saw light from a big-screen television flicker on the dull whitish walls. I rode past. It would take a few minutes to get myself ready. Had to get my mind around what I intended to do. I was there for murder. Premeditated. Cold-blooded. Murder.

Riding around the block, I realized I had a problem. The houses on both sides of the street stood close to one another. The loud blast from my 38 Special would generate calls to Johnny Law and bring nosey neighbors to their doors. I needed a new plan, a new weapon. Something quiet but effective. Looking behind the passenger seat of the Accord, I found a piece of wood. I held it in my hand for a moment and imagined swinging it down to crunch his skull, but beating him to death would take too damn long and attract attention. I put it down and opened the glove box to find a short, stout hunting knife with a sharp, pointed blade just under five inches. This would be my weapon.

The street lamp in front of the house was out, so I parked beneath it. Feeling concealed in the darkness for the moments it took me to slip on my thin gloves, I closed my eyes and breathed deeply to calm my pounding heart. I thought of Mary. Her purple hair. Her brokenness. It was time for vengeance.

I swallowed hard, took a deep breath, and slipped the blade inside my belt. I heard a train rumble and clang down its track nearby as I stepped from the car and turned my eyes toward the flickering television light coming through the large window to the left of the door. I walked up the three steps to the dark porch and looked through the window to see him sitting sloppily in a chair in front of the television. Fierce heat burned through me, filled me with the energy I'd need to slay him.

I pulled the knife from my belt, extended my shaking hand to open the screen door, and knocked. Looking through the window, I saw him. His thinning hair and stupid goatee. His head hanging at a strange angle. I knocked again. Pretty hard this time. He struggled to his feet and started toward the door. My teeth chewed at my lower lip, while I waited for him to open the door. I heard him fumble with the door knob. I saw it turn and thoughts of Mary, icy cold in her black dress, filled my mind.

When the door opened, he stood stupid-faced. I shoved him into the darkness and started slashing at his stumbling form. He retreated as I advanced, slashing the flesh of his hands and wrists. His blood flowed deep red and glistened in the television light. It dripped onto the bare

125

wood floor, and the room filled with the scent of a slaughter house. I breathed it in, and something in me snapped. Maybe it was the last strand of social constraint that had held me in check till then. All fear fell away. All concern for my life in this world or after dissipated, and rage, pure and complete, flowed through my nerves and muscles, and I stood tall above the cowering Johnson, who'd fallen back. Looking down on him, I raised my hands high above my head. I breathed in the scent of his blood and let loose with a yell so fierce and primal that he began to cry in fear for his soul. Not his life. He knew that was mine to take. He feared for his soul. That scrapheap of petty thoughts and selfish deeds. I saw the tear flow down his blood-spattered cheek and then thrust the blade deep into his chest. Deeper and deeper it went, and I fell upon him to churn the handle so the tip of the blade would shred his putrid heart. His stupid face went limp. His blood soaked into the bare wood floor and dripped into the soil below, while in the sky above, the planets moved, indifferent to the affairs of men.

35

I drove carefully through police-infested downtown and up Bardstown Road. Certain that every passing or trailing vehicle would blue light me, I kneaded the steering wheel and tried to wipe away Johnson's blood with some fast food napkins. Though the night was cool, I sweated profusely, and when I checked the mirror I saw trickles of sweat mixed with blood on my face. If the police had stopped me for any reason, I'd have been arrested, but I kept my speed down and colored between the lines like a good kindergartner.

Once in Cherokee Park, where I'd left my truck, I parked in a gravel lot next to Beargrass Creek. I wiped down the Accord and walked to a spot where the creek makes a strong bend and a huge square boulder sits in the water. I made my way across a makeshift trail of stones to the boulder and climbed on top of it. I was smeared with the blood of my enemy, but my heart was at ease, as I turned my eyes to the clear night sky. I didn't believe in God. I believed in a sort of rightness and wrongness of thought and deed in relation to one's inherent nature and deepest being. Feeling certain my deed had been right and proper in the vast and indifferent order of the universe and knowing it had been no perversion of my humanity, I raised the weapon above my head in a celebration of the vengeful slaughter. Moonlight glinted from the blade, and my heart filled with joy. I'd killed Mary's rapist. I hoped to see her again in my dreams. I hoped she would be pleased. I threw the knife far upstream, heard it splash, then jumped into the cold water.

I walked onto the bank of the creek near my truck, looked left and right, and then darted to it. Once inside, I started the truck, eased onto the curving road, and headed toward Berry Boulevard. It was nearing eight-thirty. I needed to change clothes and get some dry ammunition for my pistol. I'd go to West Haden that night to find Veronica and bring her back with me.

36

The ride to West Haden seemed much
shorter this time. I was somewhat familiar
with the terrain and landmarks and knew
what to look for. Still, I had plenty of
time to think. Johnson didn't really come
up. I wasn't bothered one bit by the memory
of what I'd done, and I took that as proof
that I'd done the right thing. Instead, my
thoughts were occupied by Veronica Rene,
her Peekaboo hair, her petite body, her
predicament. How had she fallen into
Laraunt's hands? How was she related to
Murphy? It wasn't adding up. Was she
Murphy's mistress? If so, why did
Constance care so much about her?

I pulled onto the hotel's long drive and
saw the top of the dome above the evergreen
trees. The place was old and had once or
twice fallen into decrepitude. Now it was
a pristine beauty. I parked, checked my 38
Special for ammo, and slipped it back into
my shoulder holster. Stepping from the
truck, I smoothed the front of my sports
coat. I walked toward the rear entrance.
Tingles radiated from my heart as I passed
through the door, and the hairs on the back
of my neck stood. I was here. The time had
come to face my fear. The time had come to
save Veronica Rene. I must not fail. I took
a deep breath and looked around the place.
Marble floors, meander-patterned rugs, and
beyond the entry hall, the grand dome
rising seven stories. There was no
registration desk at this entrance, and
the employees welcomed sightseers, so no

one gave me a second look. I walked into the vast space beneath the dome, heard my footsteps echo through the beehive chamber, and looked up to see the multi-colored oculus at the apex of the dome.

Taking a seat at a table near the bar, I ordered a sweet tea and began nursing it. Aware of every draft and breath, my body tingled with sensations. I noticed a woman glance at me. A tipsy redhead. A working girl perhaps. One of Laraunt's? She reminded me a little of Mary. Tender and vulnerable. I looked away. Had to stay focused. The tea was smooth-sipping and sticky sweet the way Francesca had made it. I still missed her but had made peace. I missed Mary but had avenged her death. My heart was filled with gold stars and smiley faces except one, which was partially obscured by wavy blond hair. It was desperate. Veronica was in danger.

Sitting in the echo chamber, I took a long sip of the sweet tea. Just then, I heard a strangely-familiar voice echo through the domed space. I turned my head to the right to see Veronica, struggling slightly against the much larger Doc Laraunt, who held her by the elbow. They continued toward the center of the floor, as I watched from the edge of the circular space. He tugged her arm. She resisted but was overpowered by the stronger man. Heat rose into my face, and I unbuttoned my sports coat. When they reached the center of the vast hall, the spot directly beneath the color-shifting oculus, she launched into a fit of tears and collapsed onto the floor. Standing tall above her, Laraunt tugged her arm and growled, "Get up."

"No," she cried, "I can't."

I rose from my seat and, reaching for my 38 special, started toward them. He flashed his eyes at me, locked me in his gaze, and I felt the intensity of his hateful heart. It reached out to me across that domed space to tangle with my own righteous fury, but did not have the intended effect. I did not freeze. Instead, I pulled my pistol from its holster and levelled it as he pulled his own piece. Walking toward him, I saw the flash from his muzzle and felt my body jerk to the left. The boom from his shot filled the enclosed space. It had just begun to echo when I squeezed my trigger. The pistol jumped in my hand, and the thunderous boom resounded through the hollow space. Laraunt jolted, staggered, and clutched his chest. Blood seeped through his crisp white shirt, spilled over his fingers, and dripped onto the marble floor. He collapsed to a knee and looked at me with wide eyes. Surprise faded to regret, and finally gave way to an expression of respect. Then he sprawled limp on the cold stone.

Lying in a growing pool of Laraunt's blood, Veronica shivered and cried. I knelt and took her into my arms, pressed my cheek against the crown of her head and noticed a sticky sweet floral scent with hints of vanilla. That's when all the pieces fell into place. I stroked the blond wig from her head to reveal her natural brunette hair. Looking into her eyes, I saw the blue disks of her color contacts extending beyond her natural brown irises, and my consciousness spread beyond the confines of my body to fill the domed space. It met the gaze of the color-shifting oculus above, and a wave of thrills ran through my body, as sirens drew near, and my unburdened soul glowed with the rapture of love for Mary and Francesca in my heart and Constance Murphy in my arms.

BOOK 2

Jimmie Star's stubbly cheek twitches. His brows rise up then settle back down. Slowly, he parts his eyelids, just a little, to peer through the veil of black lashes into the white glare from the light above.

He blinks and draws a long breath of dead air: bitter and antiseptic. It burns the back of his throat. He swallows hard then exhales microscopic corpses. Mitochondria. Bacilli. Tiny organic balloons deflate with tiny death cry puffs, swirl like cigarette smoke through the stale air, and then settle down onto the linoleum floor and blue curtain around the bed.

Shifting his eyes, he follows an I.V. tube down to his arm, sees the place where it enters his skin covered by a small bandage stained with dried blood. Dark red. Almost black. The I.V. had been feeding him saline and sleep, but now it's empty, and he's awake. Awake to the white light, the blue curtain, and the pain: A constant ache reaching 3.5 on his personal richter scale of suffering.

Jimmie raises his right hand to touch the tender spot just below his collar bone. Through the thin fabric of his hospital gown, he feels the loose ends of sutures. Pressing firmly, he increases the intensity of pain, feels it travel through the tissues of his body. Sliding his hand over his shoulder, he finds sutures on the back side also.

***

I've been shot. Doc Laraunt shot me. Again. I hadn't noticed in the moment but now recall the muzzle flash from his pistol and the impact rocking me. I hadn't noticed. So fierce was my determination to save Veronica Rene from that man. I leveled my Smith and Wesson, saw the muzzle cover his chest, and briefly looked into his eyes: bloodshot and glistening with malice. That's when I squeezed the trigger and felt the Smith and Wesson jolt in my hand. The boom echoed through the dome of West Haden, and I watched the expression of his eyes change from contempt to respect and regret, and red blood seeped through his crisp white shirt. With the sounds of gunshots echoing through that round space, I watched him fall onto his knees, and then onto his face. That's when I went to her. I went to Veronica Rene but found Constance Murphy, and the darkening world spun around as sirens drew near.

***

Noises startle Jimmie back to his senses. Thin blanket. White light. Blue curtain. He strains to prop himself up on his left elbow, looks in the direction of the sounds, and thinks: *Perhaps the door of this room is in that direction. If this is a hospital as it seems to be, then the doorway would give access to a network of corridors and rooms where the sick and injured receive care, and I would be one of those injured people in that building, but what do I know? Only what I perceive. A bitter scent, blue curtain, linoleum tile floor, rectangular ceiling tiles, and the sounds of two people talking.*

***

After a moment, he resolves to go to the curtain to investigate. He will locate an opening, part the curtains, and peek through. What will he find? A yawning black void? A bowling alley? Iron bars? He tries to sit up but can't quite make it. The sedatives haven't worn off completely, and he's groggy.

Again, he hears the man and woman talking. A brief exchange somewhere beyond the wall of blue fabric. He turns his head, strains to hear, but only makes out a single word, and that word, spoken in a hushed tone, is "murder."

Murder? The word stretches like taffy through his mind. Long and slow it plays out. *Murrrrderrrr*.

FADE IN:

EXT. HOUSE FACADE – NIGHT

JIMMIE STAR'S POV

JIMMIE walks along a crumbling sidewalk toward an elevated porch. Looking through a window, he sees RANDALL JOHNSON slumped in a chair before a flickering television. JIMMIE reaches out his hand to open the screen door, knocks on the entrance door with the butt of a hunting knife, and stares at the peeling paint on the door. After a long moment, we hear RANDALL working the lock inside. The door swings open to reveal a drunk and disheveled RANDALL, and JIMMIE lunges toward him.

***

Oh, yeah. That. Well, fuck it. I'll take the time. It'd be a small price to pay for seeing Johnson go down bloody. So let's get this over with.

Jimmie parts his lips and tries to speak, but his tongue sticks to the roof of his mouth until it peels loose, and he croaks, "Hey."

He stares at the curtain, but nothing happens. His call simply fades away like the work of an obscure novelist. No one pulls back the curtain, so he tries again. Book Two. This time with gusto, he yells, "HellOoo."

Footsteps scuff and tap across linoleum. A cavalry charge of uncertainty. A group of horseback Indians rides across the parched earth: brown and crisp. A cloud of dust rises and roils, and the curtain slides noisily to reveal:

Ashley Judd

Height: 5'5"
Weight: 135 lbs.
Shoe size: 8.5
Dress size: 2
Bra size: 34B
Measurements: 34-24-35
Ethnicity: White
Hair Color: Brown
Eye Color: Brown

She's a baby-faced nurse with ruddy cheeks, shiny pink lips, and wavy brown hair just below her chin.

"Well HellOoo, Jimmie Star." She caresses him with her glistening brown eyes, rests her hand on his, and squeezes it gently.

"I'm Judith, daughter of Merari, the son of Ox, the son of Joseph, the son of Ozel, the son of Elcia, the son of Ananias, the son of Gedeon, the son of Raphaim, the son of Acitho, the son of Eliu, the son of Eliab, the son of Nathanael, the son of Samuel, the son of Salasadal, the son of Israel."

"What's going on, Judith? Where am I?"

"St. Luke's. You collapsed at West Haden after you —"

Stepping from behind the curtain, a police officer interrupts. "Let's wait for the detective."

"Sure. Fine." Judith straightens Jimmie's thin blanket, "If you don't mind, officer, I'll tend to my patient now."

"Yeah. Okay. Just cut the gab. The detective will be here shortly."

Judith tucks the blanket around Jimmie, strokes his strong shoulders, and gazes into his eyes.

He focuses on her acorn-shaped face, notices the features: structurally symmetrical but different from side to side in their surface details. Her glossy brown eyes focus on him, but the left one squints a little, and the brow on that side arches slightly higher than on the other. Her lips, smooth and pink, rise a bit more at the left corner as she smiles, and her left cheek, full and rosy like the right, stands out a bit more prominently. Adding to her elegant yet homey appearance, brunette hair swoops toward her left eye to give her face a totally random shape.

Looking at her, Jimmie sees, she has two faces: Each beautiful and soft and caring but wildly different. The right shows an elegant and classic beauty, sleek and refined, while the left displays a chubbier beauty, a little drunk and lumpy, but the whole is unified by the perfection of the underlying structure: Her bones. The result is the mesmerizing beauty of deep structure. The beauty of galaxies that reveals beneath the apparent chaos and randomness an organizing principle: gravity or dark matter or deep structure or whatever. For Judith, it is not only perfect bones but also a force of will and pride, apparent in the directness of her gaze and the set of her jaw, that creates her uncanny beauty.

Her two aspects are unified by confidence so that what could have been a Cubist portrait gone awry is, to Jimmie's eyes, perfection.

He smiles.

Judith continues looking into his eyes, and Jimmie, feeling suddenly vulnerable, turns away to look around the room. He sees a square chair at the end of the bed and a vase of red roses on the window sill. He nods, rubs a hand across his eyes, and then looks back to Judith. "How long have I been here?"

"Three days. Healing. Sleeping. Dreaming."

"The roses. Who are they from?"

Jimmie watches Judith walk around the bed toward the window. *Not so much Ashley Judd. There's a little Marion Cotillard. Sweet face with a little more meat. Oh, yeah, full breasts and hips. Round and strong.*

"The card says Constance."

"Yeah." Jimmie nods. "Constance."

"The brunette?"

Jimmie raises a brow. "Yeah."

"She came to visit, but you were asleep. She stood at the end of the bed, rubbed your foot, and cried."

"So she's okay?"

"Seemed fine."

Jimmie nods.

"Y'all together?"

Jimmie shifts his eyes to meet hers, sees the blush come over her face.

"I mean, the paper said —"

"She's a client."

"She must really love you after you saved her life."

"Maybe she does, but —"

"Oh?" Judith brushes a loose thread from her scrubs.

The scuffing of shoes and a mumbling exchange between men announce the arrival of the detective.

Judith flashes her eyes toward Jimmie and smiles, then they turn toward the approaching detective, who strides across the linoleum floor like a conquering general.

"Excuse us, toots." Removing his black pork pie hat, he tilts his head toward the door. "We need a moment."

Judith glances at Jimmie, gives him a crooked smile, and walks through the door into the hallway.

"Detective Holofernes." He offers his thick hand. Jimmie squeezes the blunt fingers and beefy palm.

Holofernes looks at Jimmie with flinty blue-grey eyes, chews his lower lip, and says, "Look here, Star." He rubs his black-dye mustache. "Everything looks good on the Laraunt thing. The shooting. Clear case of self-defense. We got eyewitnesses and a deposition from Constance Murphy. Said you were working for her. Saved her life, and that seems to be true. So, that's that."

Jimmie glances toward the door for Judith but doesn't find her.

"Problem is," Detective H. presses his lips together, "got me another killing the same night." He looks into Jimmie's eyes. "A bloody stabbing. Some pervert named Randall Johnson. You know him?"

Jimmie shakes his head.

"You sure?" His cheek twitches. "Seems a neighbor saw your picture on the front page of the *Courier*. Recognized you. Said you're the one. The killer." He studies Jimmie's reaction, which is nothing. "I looked into it. Asked around. Looks like you were with a bar girl called Peaches at the time."

"Yeah. That's right. Peaches."

"Okay, you're not my guy." He drops a folded newspaper onto Jimmie's lap. "Be a shame to arrest a bona fide hero." He turns, walks toward the door, and tosses a backhand wave over his shoulder. "See ya 'round, Star."

Jimmie unfolds the paper and reads the headline:

Star Kills Laraunt

According to eyewitnesses, Louisville-based private detective Jimmie Star shot and killed alleged criminal kingpin Doc Laraunt. The two men, armed with pistols, confronted one another in the rotunda of West Haden Hotel. Laraunt fired first and struck Star in the shoulder. Star returned fire and hit Laraunt in the chest.

The coroner pronounced Laraunt dead at the scene.

Star lost conscious-ness due to blood loss, and Paramedics transported him to St. Luke's Hospital in Louisville.

"It was like an old-fashioned duel," said Steven Charles of Denver, Colorado, "They faced off, and you could see in their eyes they had beef. The woman with the big guy

(Laraunt) just laid there and cried."

Police identified the woman as Constance Murphy of Louisville and indicated she and Star knew one another.

"It's not altogether clear what was going on. It's a bit complicated," said Detective Holofernes of LMPD, "but we're pretty certain Star was working for Constance Murphy. For sure there was some shenanigans, because hotel employees knew Constance Murphy as Veronica Rene, and we don't know why. Like I said, it's complicated."

Hotel staff indicated the woman they knew as Veronica Rene had a relationship with Doc Laraunt.

"Veronica had been around for a while," said Jessica Slaughter, West Haden bartender on duty that night,

"Everyone knew she was Laraunt's girl, but she didn't seem too happy about it."

Following the shoot-out, Jimmie Star comforted Constance / Veronica and, according to Slaughter, was surprised when her blonde wig came off.

"It was a shock. You could see it in his eyes," Slaughter said, "He just sorta looked at her for a second then drooped down next to her on the floor. That's when I realized who he was. He's Jimmie Star, and he just got back."

Police refused to speculate, but the facts are that Star had been scheduled to testify against Laraunt in a prostitution and government corruption case on December 22, 2014. Two weeks before the scheduled testimony, December 8, 2014, someone shot him and his wife, Francesca, on a sidewalk in downtown Louisville.

Star's wife, Francesca died, and Star refused further involvement in the case against Laraunt.

"Everyone knows Laraunt killed his wife," said slaughter, "Everyone but the police."

***

That explains the flowers and cards and Judith's loving touches. I'm front page stuff again and have a fan club. Seems Judith is a member. Detective H. too. The way he fed me that alibi. Practically winked at me. Wonder what he's after. What card he has up his sleeve.

Judith returns, all smiles and arched brows. "Now, let's freshen you up." She reaches around Jimmie to unsnap his gown and presses her cheek, warm and smooth, against his. Blood rushes into his face, and he draws a quick breath to catch her fruity-sweet scent. He raises a hand, moves it toward the back of her leg but stops short of touching her. His fingertips linger for a moment, sense the subtle warmth from her body, and he imagines her supple flesh giving beneath his hands.

After a few seconds of leaning into Jimmie, brushing cheeks and breathing on his neck, she opens his gown and begins to remove it. He lays back, feels the thin fabric slide over his shoulders and trail across his bare chest. Judith touches his forehead lightly with her fingertips, slides them down the bridge of his nose, and his eyes fall closed. Like a submissive dog, Jimmie exposes his vital organs to her. Offers her the opportunity to hurt him. Cut his throat. Gouge out his eyes. But he knows she won't.

Just feels her good intentions. So he lays there. Naked. Eyes closed. Trusting Judith.

Soon, he hears the gentle swirling of water as she wets a sponge. He hears mellow splashing as she squeezes a small flow of water back into the pan. He waits. Every nerve ending awake and alert. Air from the overhead vent flows across his skin, gently sways the hairs on his chest. Then he feels the warm moist touch on his forehead. A thrill spreads through his body like smoke filling a bottle. His chin quivers, and he draws a sudden breath. Warm tears trickle down his cheeks and into his salt and pepper beard. He feels the spastic quaking of his stomach, listens to the irregular gasps of his breathing, and then looks up at Judith to see her gazing into his eyes. She says in a voice clear and present, "Welcome back."

2

Returning from the restroom, Jimmie finds Constance Murphy sitting in the square chair.

"Hello, Jimmie." She stands.

"Good ta see ya, Constance."

She walks to him, and he sees her tears: glistening diamonds on her smooth cheeks. Constance opens her arms and embraces Jimmie, who holds her head close to his chest. He feels her warmth through the thin hospital gown and, when he smells her fruity sweet scent, recalls the sound of his Smith and Wesson reverberating through the dome of West Haden Hotel.

Around and around the hollow space, the sonorous boom travelled. Swirling and circling, going forth and coming back like the wandering of one's mind, the explosive report swept over him and a woman. Was it Veronica? Was it Constance? He knelt to hold her in his arms and looked down into her eyes. Were they blue? Were they brown?

"Please forgive me, Jimmie, for lying to you."

"I don't blame you."

"I was so scared. I had no choice. And you came through for me. How can I thank you, Jimmie?"

"Not necessary."

"But you saved my life." She looks up into his eyes.

"And you saved mine." His voice quavers. Looking into her eyes, he notices they are brown as they had been when she first came into his office.

"Well." She nods firmly. "I'll never forget what you did for me." Reaching into her black leather purse, she pulls out a check, looks at it, and says, "It's not nearly enough but it's all I have."

She hands it to him, and when he sees that it's made out for $20,000 he says, "I can't accept this. It's too much."

"Don't insult me, Jimmie." She closes the purse and wipes the tears from her face. "My life is worth far more."

Jimmie nods.

"I only wish I could give you what you deserve." She looks at him, raises her brows.

"And what would that be?

"My heart. My soul. My undying love and devotion."

Her chin quivers, lips press together.

Reaching out, he takes her hand and gently rubs the palm and fingers.

"What about your husband, Michael?"

"Oh, no, I left him. After what he did, he deserves the worst."

"Yeah." Jimmie looks at her, takes in the lovely symmetry, elegance, and femininity of her features. He raises a hand to stroke her high cheek and trace the contour of her small chin. He sees her full lips press together and feels a sudden sternness. A harsh instinct to turn away. It's as much for her protection as for his. She is much too good, too kind and gentle for him, and he knows it.

"Thank you, Constance, but you should go now."

Tears flow down her smooth cheeks, as she brushes some wrinkles from her dress and forces a small smile. Just then, Judith walks in carrying an armload of clothes.

"'Bout ready to go?" Seeing Constance, she says, "Oh, I'm sorry. Didn't know you had company."

Wiping tears from her face, Constance says, "I was just leaving." She looks for a moment into Jimmie's eyes, turns toward the door, and from a standing position with feet beneath her shoulders and weight evenly distributed across them, Constance Murphy

- shifts her weight slightly to her right leg
  - o by moving her hips over that foot
    - ▪ using the muscles of her left leg and foot in coordination.
- She extends her left foot, clad in red patent leather pumps, forward about twelve inches and into position to receive her body weight as she
  - o leans forward slightly
    - ▪ using the muscles of her left leg and foot in coordination.
- For a moment her left foot hovers slightly above the linoleum floor, and Jimmie sees the brilliant reflections on the shoe's polished surfaces. Then
- the left heel touches the floor, and she
  - o thrusts her hip over the left foot
  - o using the muscles of her right leg and foot in coordination.
- As her right heel rises, her weight moves forward and left.
- Constance pushes forward and left with the toes of her right foot, and

- the left foot accepts the weight of her body.
    - The heel strikes first.
    - Then the toe snaps down.
- The weight of her body now supported by her left foot,

    Constance extends her right leg forward about twelve inches in front of her left in preparation to receive her weight and propel her through the doorway.

"Thought you might like some fresh duds." Judith holds out the clothes. "Your old ones were ruined."

"Blood?"

"Yeah."

Jimmie reaches out and takes the clothes, "Thanks." Looking through them, he sees stylish jeans with fancy stitching, designer underwear, and a cable knit sweater. *Very nice. I'm gonna be snazzy in these new threads.* "Guess my shoes survived?"

She chuckles. "Just barely." Bending down, she retrieves the hiking boots from beneath the bed. "Here ya go." Jimmie takes them in his hands.

"Ya know, Jimmie, you were pretty lucky. The way the bullet passed through your shoulder." She touches the entry wound with the tip of her index finger. "It went in here, just below the clavicle but above the coracoid. Pierced the skin, tore through the supraspinatus muscle, somehow missed the subclavian artery and vein, and then exited here." She touches the wound on the back of his shoulder. "Through and through." She tilts her head and looks into Jimmie's eyes. "That's what we call it."

"Yeah?"

"Yeah."

"No serious damage?"

"You'll recover fine."

"Good. I can continue my career as a great painter."

"Yeah. Smash the paradigms of depiction to reveal a new reality."

"That's what I do."

Their chuckles fade to silence and Jimmie says, "I guess this is goodbye."

"It doesn't have to be." Judith tilts her head and smiles. "I get off in ten minutes. Could give you a ride."

- "No, thanks. This is goodbye. I gotta get back to work. You know, cases to solve and bad guys to kill." (Go to chapter 3a on Page 205)
- "I'd like that. We could get to know each other. Who knows what might happen." (Continue reading chapter 3)

3

After a flyby from the doctor, Jimmie dresses in his new clothes. Then Judith escorts him down to a waiting taxi, which takes him around the corner to the nearest fast food restaurant, where he waits for her to pick him up. She had thought it would be best to keep their budding relationship a secret from her employer and coworkers, and he agreed that the fewer people who knew their business the better.

He didn't have to wait long. Maybe ten minutes. Just long enough to eat some fries and grow uncomfortable in the plastic Technicolor world of Mcthis and Mcthat. It is just too much for him. The happy music. The false smiles. The stupid ass name badges. And that incessantly-smiling clown. *What makes him so fucking happy?*

Jimmie sits in one of those chairs mounted to the table so that it won't push in or out but only turn from side to side. So that's what he does. He turns from side to side and eats fries and waits for Judith to pull up and save him from the falseness of this place. He waits and thinks of her and what they might do. Things that would make that smiling clown blush. He imagines making love to her long and slow, savoring every slippery movement, every bit of friction and resistance. Perhaps she has some pills to heighten the experience or maybe some weed. *We could get high and I'd wrap her tight in my arms and hump her good and strong and let my hands wander here and there along her curving contours. Now her shoulder. Now her ass. Now her lovely breasts. And I'd hump and grind, and she'd moan and buck, and we'd go until we were depleted and satisfied and then—the honk of a car horn, and I'm smiling like that stupid ass clown. Fucking pervert.*

Jimmie sees Judith through the window and nods. Leaving his fry bag on the table, he squeezes out of the chair and heads for the door. Pushing through it, he meets the cold air. A chill travels through him but especially focuses on his injured shoulder, which complains with sharp twinges of pain. The doctor had prescribed some pills, but Jimmie thought, *fuck that. I've been down that road before.*

He walks toward her shiny blue Accord and pulls open the door to catch the vanilla scent of her air freshener. Getting in, he lets the seat back a little and turns to see her shiny pink lips and smooth round teeth.

"Wanna stop by my place first?"

"Whatever you want."

4

Her place is in the Highlands. Just a stone's throw from Bardstown Road. A nice large house with hardwood floors and high ceilings, all done up with pastels on the walls and heavy, custom-made drapery. They stand for a moment on an Oriental rug in the foyer, then she gestures toward the living room couch and says, "Make yourself at home."

Walking toward the couch with its sleek and simple Modernist form and Greek columns at the ends, Jimmie looks around to see a floor to ceiling bookshelf packed with books and a room with hodgepodge decor. There's a Victorian globe lamp in front of an African mask and black and white Noir movie poster on the wall. A repurposed barn wood coffee table stands on a bamboo mat. He sits and looks back to Judith, still in the foyer. "Can I get you anything? Coffee?"

"Yeah. That'd be great."

'Okay. How ya take it?"

"Black is fine."

"I'll get it brewing. Don't go anywhere."

Jimmie nods and watches her go toward the kitchen, studies the firm roundness of her hips.

With kitchen noises in the background, Jimmie shuffles through a stack of magazines on the coffee table. Cosmos mostly. Pictures of beautiful women on the go. Hair blowing in an ever-present breeze. Shiny lips parted to show glistening white teeth. Headlines on keeping one's brow game strong and mind-blowing sex moves. Flipping through one, he sees page after page of advertisements for push up bras and skin toning creams and wrinkle-fighting lotions and seductive perfumes and control-top panties and chip-proof nail polish and gravity-defying conditioner and plastic surgery clinics.

Judith returns to find Jimmie knee deep in an article on what men really want in bed. She's carrying two coffee cups and wearing silk pajamas. Pink with little bits of white fur trim at the ankles and wrists.

"Thought we could stay in for a while. Hope you don't mind."

"Not at all." Looking her over, Jimmie sees her curves more clearly than before. Narrow waist. Full hips. Braless breasts moving freely behind the thin layer of shining silk. He wants to reach out and pull her to him but decides to draw the game out, build up the tension and desire, make her wait, so he takes the cups, sets them on the table and pats the couch by his side.

She curls up cozy and warm with her hands on her legs and her eyes on Jimmie. "You look really nice, Jimmie, in those clothes."

"Thank you. They fit well."

"I got your measurements while you were sleeping and shopped for them myself." She smiles, "Picked out the colors and fabrics and styles to suit you, who I thought you were. My fantasy, I guess." She smiled. "Now you're here. My fantasy man. And we're sitting side by side on my couch."

"Yeah. And what do you want? From your fantasy man?"

"Perhaps, we can make you a bit more comfortable. How 'bout you slip off your shoes?" She smiles, "That's it. Feel better?"

"Yeah." Reaching out to stroke her shoulder, Jimmie says, "I like the way the silk drapes from your shoulders and flows across your collar bones and rests on your breasts."

She strokes Jimmie's hand, as he continues.

"The way it gathers in the hollow space of your waist and stretches smooth against your thighs.

Placing his hand on the inside of her thigh, Judith leans toward him, and they kiss deeply. Little by little, they undress one another and make love. Pleasure and pain mingle, and mid-morning passes into afternoon, as they sweat and writhe on the couch and floor until exhaustion and satisfaction overtake them and they collapse in a mutual embrace.

5

It's late when they wake, and they're hungry, so Jimmie recommends going out to eat, but Judith insists on cooking for him. "I'll make lasagna and garlic bread and we'll have salad, and we can talk. I want to know all about you, Jimmie." She smiles, "Everything. And I'll tell you about myself too." She raises her brows, "My secrets."

"I'd like that, Judith."

"Please, call me Jude." Tilting her head and smiling, she takes Jimmie by the hand, "Let's shower, then I'll make dinner while you rest." She leads Jimmie upstairs. He watches her nude form ascending the steps before him. Hips and bottom shifting left and right. Desire for her stirs. He wants to take her before one of the large windows at the front of the house. He wants to make love to her for the whole world to see. Standing proud as a man. He reaches out to stroke her hip, and she turns and says, "Let's eat first."

In the bathroom, she starts the water flowing, and while they wait for it to heat up, he falls to kissing her neck and shoulders and rubbing her back, but she insists that they wait until after dinner so they have energy to make love properly.

They step into the tub and take turns washing each other with appreciative strokes. Occasionally, he slurps the water flowing from her breasts, and she presses her bottom firmly against his erection until he makes an effort to take the play further. When he does, she gives him a playful slap and tells him he has to wait. And so it goes until they are clean and horny, then they get out and dry one another.

Judith slips on a fuzzy robe and offers Jimmie a pair of flannel pajamas.

"I bought these along with the other things." She shrugs. "Just in case."

"I see." Jimmie smiles, "Anything else?"

"I have enough clothes to keep you dressed for as long as you wanna stay."

He shakes his head and laughs.

"It's totally up to you." She smiles, "I mean, I'm not forcing you." She looks into his eyes, "I just want—I want to love you. And I want you to love me."

He looks at her small before him. Something subliminal identifies her as a kindred spirit. Perhaps it's the shine of her brown eyes or her confidence and self-direction. Whatever, Jimmie feels a companionship with her, and is willing to play along and make nice.

"I'd like that, Jude."

"Now. I'll make supper. You relax on the couch. Read if you want or watch T.V. Whatever. You're home now. We can go by your office and get whatever you need or just let it rot. It doesn't matter. You don't need to work. I can support us. We're together now. This is your home, and I devote myself to you, Jimmie Star."

"Let's go downstairs. Do you have any wine?"

'We have plenty."

"Of course we do."

She leads Jimmie back to the living room, kisses him on the cheek, and says, "You take it easy, while I cook supper."

Jimmie strolls around the room. Looks through the large window to see the houses across the street and a few people walking in the last bit of daylight. His new neighbors. He takes a deep breath, lets it out slowly, and then sprawls out on the couch.

While the air fills with the aromas of cooking onions and garlic and the sounds of sizzling ground beef and a bubbling pot of pasta, Jimmie reclines on the couch. His couch. A gift from Judith. He thinks of her cooking for him. Happy to do it. He thinks of her spreading herself out for him. Happy to do it. He thinks of her professed devotion to him but feels no need or desire to test it. He trusts her and knows that whatsoever he asks she will do.

Rising to his feet, he walks to the bookshelf, where he finds an eclectic collection of volumes. Classics and horror and philosophy and college texts on Art History and literary anthologies and erotica and private detective stuff and sci-fi and books on birds and apocryphal biblical texts and on and on. He pulls out a copy of *If on a Winter's Night a Traveler* and settles down to read a book about reading a book.

Soon he's lost in the endless beginnings and the growing desire to read on.

She comes to him and, not wanting to disturb his reading, sits gently beside him until he looks up.

"Care to eat now?"

"Yes."

"Follow me." She leads him to the dining room, where she bids him sit then goes out to bring in the plates piled high with lovingly-prepared food. "Hope you like it.'

"I'm sure I will. Thank you."

Forks press through tender layers of saucy pasta. Hands tear garlic bread with crispy crust. Teeth slide across the tines of forks and chew fresh romaine lettuce and burst juicy cherry tomatoes. They eat and look at one another admiringly, and he reaches over to stroke her hand.

"This is delicious." He says, "Thank you, Jude."

She smiles. "I'll always cook for you, my darling." She smiles. "When you are finished, we can relax with some wine and talk if you like. I want to know who you are, Jimmie, so I know what you need from me, how I can help you."

6

Jimmie and Judith sit close and cozy on the couch in the dimly-lit living room. The only light shines from a torchier lamp in the corner by the bookshelves. It illuminates a circle on the ceiling, which reflects the light dimly throughout the room. The two new lovers huddle together and stroke arms and cheeks and hair, until Judith breaks the silence saying, "What do you think, Jimmie? Can we do this? Love one another."

Jimmie sits for a moment, thinks about the question. "What is love?"

"Well, it's different for everyone. Different at different times and in different places, but I think, for me and you, here and now, it's— don't you feel it? A kind of communion between us. There's something, and I think I know what it is."

"What is it?"

"A certain morality in an immoral world."

"Morality?"

"Yeah." She half smiles. "I want to tell you something I've never told anyone."

Jimmie looks into her eyes, really concentrates on the variegated yellows and browns, and realizes how seldom he'd done that or seen anyone else do that.

"I want to tell you. I think you'll be able to relate."

Jimmie nods.

"It was the first time — well, you'll understand. I was young. Just a girl. Maybe eleven or twelve. My papaw was sick. Emphysema. He was in the hospital. Near the end, and I remember going up there day after day so my mother could sit near him and do the things you do when your husband is dying."

Jimmie nods.

"Well, I would sit there and look at him, you know? Scrawny and pathetic. Knuckles and knees bulging like knots on a tree. He'd been suffering with that disease a long time. I remember he took breathing treatments from a Bennett machine. I'd hear it hissing and sighing in the spare bedroom. Then the disease got the better of him. He went in the hospital, and everyone was trying to get him to hold on, just fight it off, but I saw him suffering. Bulging eyes. Sunken cheeks. Mouth hanging open. Then everyone formed a prayer circle around him. Gonna ask God to save him, I guess. Well, I was on the end, and should have taken his hand. His pathetic, boney hand. But I just kept looking into his glazed eyes and saw no hope there. Just suffering. Just pointless suffering at the end of life. And everyone had gathered around him to pray, but I was supposed to complete the circle so the magic would work, you see? And there I was, looking into his watery eyes, and I secretly refused. No one noticed of course. Not that I'm aware. I refused to take his hand. Refused to see him suffer further. That was the first time."

"There have been others?"

Judith looks into his eyes as he comes back to the present reality, and a sense of gratitude grows in her. Tears form on her eyelids, trickle down her cheeks. She leans into him, wraps her arms around him, and says, "Thank you, Jimmie."

Shifting his gaze to her eyes, he nods. "You know what I did, right?

160

She leans her head and smiles a little. "Yeah."

"I'd rather not talk about it." He nods.

"It was the right thing, Jimmie." She smiles. "And I love you for it."

"Yeah." He chews his bottom lip. "It was necessary."

"The law — the law doesn't care about us." She clenches her teeth. "The rulers make the laws, but the laws don't protect us. They create the parameters of the game. And it's their game we play. And in their game men can rape women with little risk of punishment." She knits her brows. "Oh, sure, the police take a statement, maybe investigate a bit, but rape kits go unprocessed, and when there is a conviction the sentence is a slap on the wrist, and the woman or girl is stigmatized. It's a horrible thing, Jimmie, to be raped, to have the gift stolen."

"Yeah."

"And we need more men like you, Jimmie. More men that stand up for women and protect us." She raises her brows. "So, to thank you, I devote myself to you, Jimmie Star. I want to make your dreams come true. What is your secret dream?"

"My secret dream?"

"Yeah. Everybody has one. What did you want to do when you were young? What was your dream?"

"I wanted to be an artist."

"Really? A painter? Sculptor? What?"

"It didn't matter. I just wanted to create. I wanted to bring imagination into reality and possibly make something that would secure my immortality."

"You wanted to live forever."

"Yeah. Through my artistic creations. I used to paint. Back in high school. Won lots of awards. Then, when I was in college, I shifted to writing. Spent my college career learning to write well."

"And what happened to that dream?"

"I don't know. Just sort of lost sight of it in the daily grind of making a living." He half smiles. "I still remember a poem I wrote several years ago."

"What?! Oh, my god, Jimmie, can you tell me? I gotta hear it."

"I don't know. It's been a long time."

"You can do it, Jimmie. For me."

"Okay, I'll try." He closes his eyes for a moment then begins.

Psychic Surgery on the Living Room

Confined and confounded

between the corners of this stale room,

I push my fingertips through the layers

of off white and eggshell and tan

to puncture the paper

and penetrate the plaster

and tear out a chunk

of the barrier between here and gone.

Darkness creeps through the void

to bind my vigor,

blur my vision,

blunt the edge of reason,

and the T.V., laughing falsely,

beckons me to float in the easy chair

on the sea of hopes and dreams of youth now

faded,

and I, feeling the shame of life wasted

in fear and despair,

summon the strength

to smash that blithering bastard.

and I, crossing the ruined room,

throw open the door, and stand

on the threshold of possibility.

"Oh, my God, Jimmie. That was great. You really are good. Here's what I want you to do. I want you to write the story of what happened at West Haden. Start at the beginning and tell it all. Think you can do that?"

"I don't know. I mean it's been a long time since I've written anything."

"Take all the time you need. Just start and don't quit. Keep at it until you make your dream come true." She strokes his cheek. "I'm here to help you."

"I'll think about it."

"No. Jimmie, I want you to do it. Commit to it."

"That might take a long time."

"We have time."

"And I have the check from Constance Murphy. Twenty grand should keep us flush for a while."

"So, what's the hold up? You'll start tomorrow?"

"I guess I could sketch out a few ideas. Jot down some memories."

"Write a novel."

"Yeah." He smiles. "I can write a novel. And what is your dream?"

"My dream is simple, Jimmie. I want you to love me."

"And what does that mean?"

"Make me feel safe in this world. Walk by my side and hold me close. When there's a noise in the middle of the night, I want you to investigate it. I want you to accept me as I am and commit to grow old with me. No matter what. I want to live as one with you and die when you die. Not a day later."

The two embrace in the dim light of their home, and hold one another until sleep overcomes them.

7

Jimmie sleeps late. When he wakes on the couch of his new home, he hears strange sounds coming from upstairs. Sitting up, he stretches and yawns and looks around until he recalls himself and his situation. He is Jimmie Star, and he lives with Judith. What's her last name? He'll find out today. First he wants to investigate the noises from the second floor, so he climbs the stairs and turns right to find an open door. Looking through it, he sees Judith, as lovely as he recalled, positioning a desk in front of a window. She turns to see him, smiles, and then gestures to the room around her.

"Like it?"

Jimmie looks around the room to see a roll-top desk with an old drafting lamp on top and a laptop computer on the workspace. An old-fashioned slat-back chair and another, more comfortable, chair in the corner. A pen and pad of paper sit next to a bottle of bourbon on a small table beside it.

"Your writing room."

"Oh, Jude. I don't know what to say."

"Just say you like it."

"I love it. Thank you."

"Now, write me a masterpiece." She smiles. "Start today. Don't wait. Start right now. I'll leave you alone. The computer's all set up with a word processing program. Just go for it."

"Well, I guess I could."

"Nonsense. You can. First thing you need is a pseudonym. A name you can hide behind. That way you can tell the truth."

"Okay. Okay. I'll do it." Jimmie rubs his hands together. "I'll do it."

Looking around, he chooses to sit in the corner chair and, taking the pen in hand, starts the crucial task of choosing a pen name. After an hour or so he devises a complex algorithm involving family maiden names and comes up with the nom de plume "A. Henry Keene" and sets pen to paper in his first effort to write a novel.

JUDITH

_____

A play in five acts

* * *

Cast of Characters

JIMMIE STAR – *Real-life detective turned aspiring writer.*

JUDITH – *Mercy-killing nurse turned lover and patron of JIMMIE STAR.*

J.C. – *JIMMIE STAR's fictional self-representation.*

CONSTANCE MURPHY – *J.C.'s client.*

DETECTIVE HOLOFERNES – *Police detective investigating the murder of Randall Johnson.*

DOC LARANUT – Criminal Kingpin.

VERONICA RENE – Missing woman.

REDHEADED WOMAN - A pleasant distraction.

<u>Act 1</u>

<u>Scene 1</u>

SETTING: Stage right - a desk, slat-
          back chair, and a large
          window with tree foliage
          visible beyond.

AT RISE: Stage right - JUDITH stands
          next to JIMMIE STAR.

JUDITH

(wearing nurse's scrubs.)

You can do it, honey.

JIMMIE STAR

Yeah. I guess.

JUDITH

Just start and don't give up. No
matter what happens, you must finish
your novel. I'll take care of
everything. Just write. Make your
dream come true. Become a writer.

JIMMIE STAR

But I'm a private detective.

JUDITH

That was yesterday. Today you begin
the transformation. Tell your story.
Write it well, and you will become a
writer. I am here to guide and

protect you. I'll do anything to make your dream come true, Jimmie, but I can't do it for you, so sit down, have a drink, and write. Begin at the beginning. Constance Murphy walks in or whatever. Don't worry. Just write.

JIMMIE STAR

(sits at desk.)

JUDITH

(kisses his cheek)

I'll leave you to it.

JIMMIE STAR

(sits and drinks and thinks.)

(Gradually, lights come up on the sides and back of the stage to reveal the facades of concrete block buildings, utility poles, and swooping powerlines. Various characters, including J.C., Mary, Constance Murphy, Doc Laraunt, Veronica Rene, and the ghosts of Francesca and Randall Johnson, wander around the stage and soon exit. All except J.C. and Constance Murphy. They remain on stage.)

(Lights illuminate a grimy plate glass door and an old oak desk and chair at center stage. This is J.C.'s office.)

J.C.

(enters the office and sits in the
oak office chair.)

JIMMIE STAR

(bends his head over his desk and
begins to write.)

J.C. is not the typical square-jawed
hero. He's got some problems. Drugs.
Booze. A guilty conscience. He's down
and out. Living in the back of his
office. Snorting Oxi off his desk.

J.C.

(drinks from a bottle of bourbon,
messes up his hair and clothes, and
applies makeup to give himself the
appearance of stubble. He snorts
something off his desk and slumps in
his office chair.)

JIMMIE STAR

But why? Why is he in such bad shape?
That's part of the story. It's the
pain in his chest. He has a bullet
next to his heart. I'll get to that.
First I want a Noir beginning. The
woman walks in. The mysterious woman.
She's small. Petite. Wearing dark
clothes. A grey pea coat. Brunette
hair. That's very important. She has
brunette hair and brown eyes.

CONSTANCE

(enters stage, walks toward the door
to J.C.'s office and pushes through
it. A brass bell rings.)

J.C.

(struggles to wake and sees CONSTANCE
standing before him. The two stare at
one another.)

JIMMIE STAR

(pours another drink.)

Now what happened? What did I say?
Does it matter what I really said? It
was probably something stupid like
"Where did you come from?" Some shit
like that. I don't know. Guess it
really doesn't matter what I actually
said. It's gotta make a good story.
Maybe J.C. says —

J.C.

Hiya, toots.

JIMMIE STAR

Oh, god, no. Maybe. Maybe he just
kinda looks at her and drifts back to
sleep. Yeah. That's it.

J.C.

(looks at CONSTANCE and
lowers his head again.)

JIMMIE STAR

Then she says something snarky. She gets kinda shitty. Just a little.

CONSTANCE

Oh, don't mind me. I'll just stand here and watch you sleep.

JIMMIE STAR

No. No. She says—

CONSTANCE

Thank goodness for G.P.S.

JIMMIE STAR

Yeah, cause she's East End. Has no idea about Berry Boulevard. Yeah.

CONSTANCE

Didn't know this part of town existed.

J.C.

Land of utility poles and cell towers.

JIMMIE STAR

But he slurs it.

J.C.

(repeats line, slurring)

JIMMIE STAR

Yeah. And she's starting to worry that maybe J.C. can't help her. But she's desperate.

CONSTANCE

Is this a bad time? I can come back.

J.C.

No. No. I just need coffee.

J.C.

(drinks deeply from a mug.)

Now, where were we? Please have a seat.

CONSTANCE

(curls up in the oak chair across the desk.)

J.C.

(studies her, as images project on a screen: Michael Kors handbag, Steve Madden heels. CONSTANCE's legs in black stockings.

CONSTANCE

(clears her throat.)

J.C.

(lights a cigarette.)

What can I do for you, Miss?

CONSTANCE

Misses.

J.C.

Of course.

CONSTANCE

Murphy. Constance Murphy.

(Image of sparkling wedding ring.)

I'm worried. Mr. Star. I'm worried about a lady friend. She's caught up in something.

J.C.

Something?

CONSTANCE

Something dangerous.

CONSTANCE

(takes an envelope from her purse and slides it across the desk.)

J.C.

(opens the envelope to find several photographs.)

(Projected images: various photos of a blonde beauty: Veronica Rene.)

JUDITH

(enters stage and

walks to JIMMIE STAR.)

(J.C.'S office, Berry Boulevard set,
and projection screen go dark.)

How's it going, honey? Making
progress?

JIMMIE STAR

Yeah. Coming right along. I'm really
getting into it. Every detail as it
happened, and everything is starting
to come together. Starting to think I
really can do this. Make a new life
for myself. Become a writer.

JUDITH

Good. I knew you could do it.
Anything I can do for you?

JIMMIE STAR

I'm good. Thanks. Really need to get
back to it.

JUDITH

(rubs JIMMIE STAR's shoulders.)

Listen. I just got a call from a
friend of ours.

JIMMIE STAR

Who's that?

JUDITH

Detective Holofernes.

                    JIMMIE STAR

        (stands and turns to face the window
        through which he sees tree foliage
                rustling in a breeze.)

Really? How did he know I was here?

                      JUDITH

I don't know, but he wants to talk to
you.

                    JIMMIE STAR

About what?

                      JUDITH

He wouldn't say, but I can guess.

                    JIMMIE STAR

Yeah.

                      JUDITH

He's coming by later.

                    JIMMIE STAR

Yeah.

            (Video plays on screen. A knife
                slashes through flesh.
            A body falls. Bloody hands.)

CURTAIN FALLS

ACT 2

SCENE 1

SETTING: Living room. Grey couch.
            Book shelves. Large doorway
            on left.

AT RISE: JIMMIE STAR sits on the
            couch. JUDITH, curled up
            next to him, rests her head
            on his chest.

                    JUDITH

I'm so happy for you, Jimmie. All the
progress you're making on the novel.
Seems you really were born to write.

                 JIMMIE STAR

Yeah. It's coming along pretty well.
I really feel I'm becoming the person
I was meant to be.

                    JUDITH

That's what I want to hear. Your
dream is coming true.

                 JIMMIE STAR

Got the Constance character all
figured out. Her motivation. She's
scared of what Doc Laraunt will do
with her. The things he will make her
do if her husband doesn't come
through with the money he owes
Laraunt. But she couldn't come clean

with me. With the private detective.
She was too proud, and he was too
messed up to see through her story.

JUDITH

Is that what happened?

JIMMIE STAR

Yeah. She came into my office and
offered me a missing person case. But
the missing person was her alter ego,
Veronica Rene. And the whole time she
hoped I'd kill Laraunt. She knew
about my wife, Francesca. She knew
Laraunt had killed her, but I was too
far gone to see how she was playing
me. I don't blame her though. She was
desperate, and I was her only hope.

JUDITH

And you came through for her.

JIMMIE STAR

Yeah, but not so much for Mary.

JUDITH

Who's Mary?

JIMMIE STAR

She was a bar girl I fell in love
with. I guess it was love. We were
junkies so there's no telling. She
introduced me to heroine, and we used

together until I cleaned up. But she
kept using and drinking and whatever
else she was doing. She was going
down fast, and I knew it but couldn't
bring myself to stop her. Then I took
her to the Hyatt, where we got a
room. She wanted to shoot up. I
couldn't watch, so I turned my back
and let her shoot a fatal dose.

                    JUDITH

Oh, honey, it wasn't your fault.

                 JIMMIE STAR

I don't know if I blamed myself at
the time, but her death filled me
with sorrow and rage. You see,
someone had done her wrong and sent
her life off course. I blamed him:
Randall Johnson. He deserved to die.

                    JUDITH

What did you do?

                 JIMMIE STAR

I stole a car and drove it to his
place in Portland. Found a hunting
knife in the car. Just right for the
job. Sharp and pointed. I took that
knife and walked up to his door. I
knocked and waited. He didn't come
straight away, so I stood there and
stared at the old wooden door. I

studied the cracked white paint for patterns and portents but found only the indifference of natural processes: expansion and contraction. Then I heard him working the lock, and adrenaline surged through my body. Adrenaline and visions of Mary, lying cold and still on the hotel bed, Barbie-doll pretty in her casket. The door swung back, and I saw his drunken face for the first time in real life. I saw his wide eyes, crooked brows, and parted lips. The face Mary had seen while he was raping her. I knocked him off balance and swung the blade through the darkness of his front room to slash his cheek. The flesh parted, and blood flowed like syrup on a stack of pancakes. I tried again for his neck, but he'd raised his hands in defense, so the blade cut his wrist, and his fingers jerked back when the blade severed his tendons. Instinctively, he pulled his hand back, and I swung again. This time the sharp edge of the blade slit his throat, opened a gaping hole, and blood spewed like water from the Falls Fountain. He clutched his neck, and I stabbed his chest with all my might. The tip pierced his sternum, and the blade disappeared. He fell back onto the hardwood floor, and I landed on top

of him to churn the handle so the tip
of the blade would shred the putrid
heart within his chest.

(They fall silent and sit
together until there is
a knock at the door.)

JUDITH

The detective.

(JIMMIE STAR nods and
JUDITH hugs him.)

Don't worry, honey.

JUDITH

(exits through the large doorway to
the foyer, where she opens the front
door and welcomes DETECTIVE
HOLOFERNES, wearing a leather
Pork pie hat.)

DETECTIVE HOLOFERNES

My, you look nice, Ms. Schein.

JUDITH

Well, thank you, detective. What can
I do for you?

DETECTIVE HOLOFERNES

I understand JIMMIE STAR is staying
with you.

JUDITH

That's right.

DETECTIVE HOLOFERNES

Think I might have a word with him?

JUDITH

Of course. He's in the living room.
Follow me.

(JUDITH and DETECTIVE HOLOFERNES
enter through the large doorway.)

JIMMIE STAR

Detective, what can I do for you?

DETECTIVE HOLOFERNES

(removes his hat and runs his fingers
through his hair.)

If you'll excuse us, JUDITH. We need
a little privacy.

JUDITH

Certainly.

(JUDITH walks through the large
doorway but stops
just outside to eavesdrop.)

JIMMIE STAR

What's this about?

DETECTIVE HOLOFERNES

I just wanted to touch base with you
concerning my investigation. You
know, Randall Johnson.

JIMMIE STAR

Yeah.

DETECTIVE HOLOFERNES

There have been a couple new
developments. Another eye-witness has
come forward. A woman that happened
to be driving by Big Rock the night
of the murder just as someone threw
something shiny into the water. We
sent a team down there to search for
the murder weapon, but they didn't
come up with anything. You know why,
Jimmie?

JIMMIE STAR

(shakes his head.)

DETECTIVE HOLOFERNES

(reaching into his inside jacket
pocket, pulls out a plastic baggy
with a hunting knife inside.)

I beat them to it.

JIMMIE STAR

(raises a hand to rub his cheek.)

I don't understand.

DETECTIVE HOLOFERNES

Sure you do, Jimmie. I have the
knife. The one you used to kill
Randall Johnson.

(They look at one another.)

Bet it has your prints all over it.
DNA. Shit like that.

DETECTIVE HOLOFERNES

(casually waves the knife in the
air.)

It'd be a shame for this to fall into
the wrong hands. Yes, sir, a cryin'
shame. So we're gonna make a little
deal. You and me.

JIMMIE STAR

What kinda deal?

DETECTIVE HOLOFERNES

I have a little side business that
could use a man like you to tie up
loose ends. Someone rough and mean
that aint afraid of the sound of
breaking bones. Someone that aint
afraid to kill.

JIMMIE STAR

I see.

DETECTIVE HOLOFERNES

Well, I hope you do, JIMMIE. I've got
you by the short and curlies, and
you'll do as I say.

JIMMIE STAR

And if I don't?

DETECTIVE HOLOFERNES

You can say goodbye to the sweet
life. No more shackin' up with Nurse
Goodbody. Say goodbye to this cozy
cottage. Say hello to Luther Luckett.

JIMMIE STAR

Yeah.

DETECTIVE HOLOFERNES

(puts the knife back into his
pocket and walks toward the
large doorway.)

I'll be in touch.

DETECTIVE HOLOFERNES

(exits the living room and finds
JUDITH in the foyer. He looks her
over, nods appreciatively, and then
hands her a card.)

Here ya go, toots. Gimme a call when
you get tired of playing house with
this bozo.

JUDITH

(takes the card and opens the front
    door for the DETECTIVE. When he
    leaves, she goes to JIMMIE STAR.)

JIMMIE STAR

What am I gonna do, Jude? He's got
the goods on me.

JUDITH

Leave him to me.

JIMMIE STAR

Just when I was starting to dream of
another kind of life. Here, with you.

JUDITH

Don't worry. Just tend to your
writing. I'll take care of
Holofernes. Trust me.

CURTAIN FALLS

ACT 3

SCENE 1

SETTING: Three sides of stage depict
            exterior of the Clarke
            Motel. Dingy tan paint.
            Doors and windows. To left
            is a sign that reads RENTAL
            OFFICE. Center stage, in
            darkness, is the interior
            of a room. Bed with
            nightstands and lamps.

BEFORE
RISE: JUDITH walks in front of
            curtain.

JUDITH

(uses a cell phone to make a call.)

(Sound of telephone ringing.)

DETECTIVE HOLOFERNES

(off stage)

Holofernes.

JUDITH

Detective? It's Judith Schein.

DETECTIVE HOLOFERNES

(off stage)

Hey, toots, I was just thinking of you.

                    JUDITH

Nothing bad, I hope.

               DETECTIVE HOLOFERNES

                   (off stage)

Could be.

                  (They laugh.)

                    JUDITH

Listen, I'd like to see you. Tonight.

               DETECTIVE HOLOFERNES

                   (OFF STAGE)

You name it. Time and place.

                    JUDITH

Clarke Motel on Dixie. Seven O'clock.

               DETECTIVE HOLOFERNES

                   (off stage)

You got it, toots.

                  JIMMIE STAR

          (walks to JUDITH in front Of
                   curtain.)

                    JUDITH

You must not ask me, Jimmie, where
I'm going tonight. I will not tell
you.

JIMMIE STAR

I see you have sandals on your feet
and bracelets on your wrists and
you're wearing chains and rings and
earrings, and I smell the delightful
scent of lotions on your skin. You
are decked out to seduce, but I don't
know who and will not ask.

JUDITH

It is best that you don't know what I
aim to do, but believe me, Jimmie,
when I have completed my task we will
be free to live and love as we see
fit. So, my darling, wish me luck.

(The two embrace and exit opposite
sides of the stage.)

AT RISE: DETECTIVE HOLOFERNES,
           carrying two bottles,
           enters the stage through
           the rental office door. He
           walks jauntily to the front
           of the stage.

DETECTIVE HOLOFERNES

(between drinks)

It is right and proper that I should
have his woman. To the victor goes
the spoils, and I have played the
game to perfection. That bungling
fool, Jimmie Star, never stood a

chance. Not only will I make love to
his woman any way I please, but I
will make her my own. Oh, you
disapprove, gentle audience? I offend
your delicate sensibilities? Well,
what would you have me do? Let him
walk scot free? Get away with murder?
It was a bloody affair. He hacked
Randall Johnson to death with this
knife. What's that? Justice, you say?
Let the courts decide the matter.
Pish posh. The only justice I see is
what a man makes for himself. You'll
see the proof for yourself.

(lights come up to reveal the room
interior at center stage.)

DETECTIVE HOLOFERNES

(enters the room, checks himself
in a mirror, and settles onto
the bed to drink and wait.
He pulls out his phone and texts.)

(sound of text alert)

JUDITH

(enters the stage. She takes out her
cell phone and looks at it, then,
looking left and right, walks to the
front of the stage.)

Room twelve. Okay, so that's where
I'll do it.

(She reaches into her purse, pulls
out a pill, and holds it up
for the audience to see.)

This should do the trick. I'll drop
this little beauty in his drink and
do what I must.

JUDITH

(skulks toward room twelve. When she
reaches the door, she takes a deep
breath, lets it out in a huff,
and knocks.)

DETECTIVE HOLOFERNES

(checks himself in the mirror
then goes to open the door.)

Judith, you look amazing. Please,
come in. Would you like a drink? Hope
you like red wine.

JUDITH

Yes. That would be nice.

DETECTIVE HOLOFERNES

(opens the second bottle of wine,
pours two glasses, and goes to
JUDITH.)

You are stunning.

JUDITH

(runs her fingers through her hair)

Well, thank you, DETECTIVE.

DETECTIVE HOLOFERNES

(sets the glasses on a table,
takes JUDITH in his arms,
and buries his face in her hair.)

What is that fragrance? So deep and
alluring. It flows over me, swallows
me.

JUDITH

(drops the pill into one of
the glasses.)

DETECTIVE HOLOFERNES

(growing excited, paws at JUDITH
aggressively.)

JUDITH

(pulls away.)

Woo, big fella, let's enjoy the
moment.

(She hands the DETECTIVE
the glass with
the pill in it and
proposes a toast.)

Here's to cunning and manipulation.

DETECTIVE HOLOFERNES

(a little wobbly already,

looks at JUDITH for a
moment then smiles.)

Sure. Cunning and manipulation.

                  JUDITII

   (sips from her glass and watches as
   HOLOFERNES gulps his glass empty.)

Now, where were we?

                  JUDITH

I was admiring your skill. The way
you played Jimmie Star.

            DETECTIVE HOLOFERNES

Guess you're playing him too for what
he's worth.

                  JUDITH

Aint much. Constance Murphey gave him
a chunk of money. I'll get that, but
you got him by the balls. He's ready
to kill on your word. How'd you
manage that?

            DETECTIVE HOLOFERNES

Didn't take much. When I pulled
Johnson's jacket I found the old rape
charge filed by Star's newly-deceased
girlfriend and figured Star for the
murder. There's just a few
motivations for a murder as brutal as

that: intense emotion. Love. Hate.
Whatever.

> (He stumbles slightly and
> blinks as he tries to
> regain his bearings.)

JUDITH

You look a little tired. Sit. Let's
talk about us. How we can bleed that
freak.

DETECTIVE HOLOFERNES

> (pulls the knife from his inside
> jacket pocket and shows it.)

Then I found this beauty.

JUDITH

Brilliant. This is it? The murder
weapon?

DETECTIVE HOLOFERNES

> (hands the knife to JUDITH with an
> exaggerated movement of his
> arm and, nearly falling,
> slurs the next lines.)

That's it. Star killed Johnson with
this knife.

JUDITH

And now I will kill you with it.

DETECTIVE HOLOFERNES

Ahh, that's the game.

JUDITH

I'm going to cut off your head.

(She leads him to the bed,
where he struggles to embrace her.)

DETECTIVE HOLOFERNES

How 'bout a kiss, Judith? Just one
kiss before I die?

(He passes out. JUDITH lays
him back on the bed and, walking to
front and center,
addresses the audience.)

JUDITH

My aim is almost achieved. I will
thrust the blade of this knife
through his neck. I will take the
head of Holofernes, place it in that
wicker basket, and carry it home to
my beloved. With the detective gone,
we will be free to live and love one
another, and when Jimmie's
transformation is complete, when he
has become a writer, I will place
this hat upon his head.

(She walks to HOLOFERNES and, leaning
over him, thrusts the knife twice
toward his neck.)

CURTAIN FALLS

SETTING: JIMMIE'S writing room as in first act.

AT RISE: JIMMIE STAR paces and drinks from a bottle of bourbon.

JIMMIE STAR

Judith has gone to kill Holofernes.

(He drinks.)

That's the only possibility. Where else would she have gone? Dressed to the nines and smelling so sweet. She has gone to kill that bastard and free us to live and love. She has gone to make my dream of becoming a writer a possibility, and, so, I must make that possibility a reality. I must justify her sacrifice. The sacrifice of her self-conception. Sure, she has killed before but only from a pure and caring heart. But this. This would be murder, cold and calculated, and so different from the mercy killings of her past. Her soul will surely suffer for it.

(He drinks.)

Well, what is a soul but memory and imagination and judgement and emotion all bound up? And what is God but what happens without our effort when we aren't looking? Paint dries. Grass grows. Things fall apart and come together aimlessly. Processes, driven by natural forces, run their courses without the least input from little ol' me. That combined with some inherent sense of right, something universal to all mankind, is what we call God, and, so, Judith killing Holofernes is, for me, somewhat akin to an act of God, coming as an act in a chain of causation. The result of a natural process of action and reaction driven by her sense of moral decency and goodness. It's what drives us, moves us through our lives. Just as gravity pulls a loose apple to the ground, and maggots consume a corpse without thinking, Judith has killed Holofernes from the goodness of her heart.

(He drinks.)

But that's not quite right. She had a choice. She's not an apple or mindless animal, and, so, she may struggle with the justification of her act. Murder cannot be taken lightly. It cannot be a mere means to enforce one's will and values, and it always leaves some trace, some stain

and taint, regardless of the absence
of a judging God. But –

(He drinks.)

I killed Randall Johnson and Doc
Laraunt, and I feel fine. Some people
just deserve to die. Some people
through their actions transgress
against the inherent and fundamental
core of human decency to the point
that rehabilitation is not an option.
Some people have just gone too far
afield, done too much damage to
others. They've lost their humanity
and prey on innocents. Driven by
greed and lust and the fear of their
own suffering, they become monsters.
Dwelling on the fringes of decent
society, they exploit the weak for
their own gain and ruin lives through
their brutality. Yes, they are
monsters to be slain for the sake of
all mankind. Was Holofernes such a
monster? Did his transgression rise
to that level of evil? His offense:
attempting to exploit and control me
for his own gain and in the process
stifling my efforts to fulfill my
destiny are evils not much different
from the pimp and drug pusher and
slaveholder. Negating another's free
will through coercion or outright
force is high crime. Coercion must be

fought tooth and nail. But murder?
Can one justify murder as a means to
gain freedom from oppression? Wars
have been fought for this very
reason. Our Revolutionary War. The
Civil War either as a response to
federal overreach or to end slavery
was about armed resistance to
coercion. So, if the past can justify
present action, then Judith killing
Holofernes is fully justified in the
pursuit of liberty.

JIMMIE STAR

(sits and writes.)

JUDITH

(walks to center front of
stage holding the
hat of Holofernes,
pauses to watch JIMMIE
as he writes, and then
continues across and
off the stage.)

JIMMIE STAR

(writes and drinks)

As light and dark cycle beyond the
window, and seasons pass, various
characters from his work-in-progress
interact on the stage. Images of West
Haden Hotel, drug paraphernalia,

knives, guns, and graves appear on the screen, and bits of dialog fill the air. JIMMIE paces and writes and interacts with characters. From time to time JUDITH enters with food, which he largely ignores, and bourbon, which he quickly consumes. Hunched over his desk, JIMMIE writes until he has finished *Peekaboo*, then rises from his chair with the completed manuscript in hand. He looks proudly toward the audience then exits.)

CURTAIN FALLS

ACT 5

SCENE #1

SETTING   Slightly misty interior of West Haden Hotel. A large domed space with marble columns, a color-changing oculus at the apex, and, at ground level, two small round tables with chairs to the left. A REDHEADED WOMAN sits at one of the tables.

BEFORE
RISE: JIMMIE sits in a wingback chair to front left of curtain and JUDITH sits in a wingback chair to front right of curtain. She is reading JIMMIE's manuscript.

AT RISE: J.C., looking haggard and anxious, walks into the marble-floored space. As the echo from his footsteps fades, he looks around and rubs the back of his neck. He glances up to the oculus then takes a seat at a table to look over the open space.

REDHEAD

                    (sips her drink and glances
           toward JIMMIE. She tosses her hair a
           bit and bounces her satin-stockinged
            leg until she finally catches his
           eye, and they look at one another.)

                        DOC LARAUNT

                    (enters the rotunda holding
           VERONICA forcefully by the elbow.)

                        VERONICA

                    (whimpers as she struggles,
                    slightly at first then more
                    vigorously as they near the
                    center of the domed space.)

                        J. C.

                    (unbuttons his sports coat.)

                        VERONICA

           (collapses in tears at center stage.)

                        DOC LARAUNT

                    (jerks her arm.)

           Get up.

                        VERONICA

           No. I can't.

                        J.C.

(rises from his seat and starts
toward them, as he pulls his 38
Special from inside his jacket.)

DOC LARAUNT

(locks eyes with J.C. but is
surprised when J.C. keeps coming. He
draws his own weapon and fires a
quick shot that rocks J.C. and fills
the space with a resounding boom.)

J.C.

(returns fire.)

DOC LARAUNT

(staggers and clutches his chest.
Blood flows through his starched
white shirt, and he collapses to one
knee. He looks into J.C.'s eyes then
sprawls limp on the cold stone.)

J.C.

(goes to VERONICA. He takes her into
his arms to comfort her. He strokes
her blond hair and finds that it is a
wig. He removes it to reveal brunette
hair. With surprise, he says,)

Constance?

(then collapses next to CONSTANCE
MURPHY.)

(The sound of approaching sirens.)

CURTAIN FALLS

                    JUDITH

        (crying, closes the manuscript,
              picks up the leather
          pork pie hat, and walks to
      center front to embrace JIMMIE.
              She places the hat
                on his head.)

3a

Jimmie took a taxi to his office on Berry Boulevard and settled back into the routines of work. Business was good. Everyone needed a hero, and Jimmie found he was a new man. Gone was the oppressive weight of guilt. Gone was the unconscious drive to destroy himself. He'd redeemed himself, but there is always some regrettable past action that starts the gears of guilt grinding. So it happened that Jimmie Star looked through the grimy plate glass to see the barren darkness of Berry Boulevard. Grey concrete, black asphalt. No color. Anywhere. The road itself, greasy and pockmarked, flowed into crumbling grey lots where the silhouettes of rectangular buildings sat heavy and black. Behind them, the bony black lattice of a transmission tower and the zig-zags of leafless trees rose into the grey sky. In front, a tall figure in black moved across the oil-slick expanse of Berry Boulevard. He could tell it was a woman. There was no mistaking the hourglass figure of this one.

Her black silhouette approached, and Jimmie's mind drifted back to Michael Murphy. His eyes: large, pleading, and black with fear. The feeling of his warm guts in his bare hand.

The ringing of the brass bell on his door startled him, and he turned to see the woman in black standing before him. Her long skirt, trimmed with an intricate lace pattern of stars and moons, clung to the arc of her hips before disappearing behind a wool pea coat tailored to accentuate her full breasts.

"Mr. Star?"

When she looked at him through the veil, he could see her face was a perfect oval and her eyes were an exotic, intoxicating blue surrounded by long black lashes.

"Mr. Star?"

"Call me Jimmie."

She extended a hand toward him. Every finger had a ring. Diamonds and emeralds and rubies. No cheap clusters. Big rocks, sparkling and flashing in the light from the buzzing fluorescent. "Elaine Bettencourt."

He took her hand, felt the slender softness of her fingers.

"What can I do for you?"

Behind the veil, the dark red outline of her lips produced a persimmon luscious voice. "My husband." She swallowed hard. "My husband is dead."

His heart fluttered. Maybe it was the Four Roses. Maybe it was the weed. Whatever. A rush of emotion spread through his body when she said that. He pressed his lips together and motioned for her to sit in the old oak chair in front of his desk. He sat on the good guy side and waited for her to continue, but she didn't. She just sat there long enough for him to take several anxious breaths and really feel the heaviness of her presence. Something about her captivated him. Was it her veil or her voice or the long lines of her curvy figure? Jimmie couldn't say, but one thing was certain. He would do as she asked.

"Killed himself." Tears formed on her eyelids. When she blinked, they rushed down her cheeks like shooting stars glistening in the night sky.

"Shot himself through the ear." She took a deep breath. "I found him in his study. Blood on the wall. Blood on the floor. Blood on his white shirt. I'd been nagging him to at least change his clothes. He surprised me when he put on the white button up. It was so, I don't know, formal." She fell silent for a second. "Anyway, he'd been bothered. Depressed. Nervous. I don't know why. Maybe he had a secret. Maybe he broke. Kept talking about static. He heard static." She pulled a small cream-colored envelope from her black clutch. "Found this under his pillow."

Jimmie took the envelope and studied it. Nice, heavy paper inscribed with blue ink, "Elaine." The letters were shaky, and there was a water stain on the paper. A small splash. He suspected it was a teardrop but didn't mention the fact.

Opening the envelope, he slid out a single piece of matching paper. Folded once. Crisply folded. He set the envelope aside face down and read.

> *Dearest Elaine,*
>
> *I can't take it anymore. This damned static. It hisses like channel zero. Squeals like short wave radio. It cuts through me like an x-ray and growls like a robotic dog digging through my mind. It uncovers my worst memories. Like the corpse. Its taut face haunts me. I shouldn't have given it to them. No matter how much they offered. Now look at me. A victim of my*

own greed. I knew what they would do. I knew the fanatics would try to kill all us wayward souls. I just didn't believe it would work, but this pistol is proof. This pistol and this damned noise. Crackling static. Fucking nonsense and guilt drive me to my death.

J.B.

"J.B.?"

"James Bettencourt."

"Oh." He scribbled the name in a small spiral notebook and returned his attention to the widow.

She nodded and said, "Something drove him to it. The static. I want to know what it is."

"Sounds like raving. Was he under some sort of strain? Work perhaps?"

"No. He was in appropriations for the museum. J.B. Speed. Not much stress there."

"Everything okay at home?"

"Yes. I mean until he withdrew. Jimmie, I want to know about the static." She pointed to the letter. "He said it drove him to his death."

"Nonsense and guilt," He corrected her. "What was his guilt? Had to do with a corpse?" He was hooked. "I'll need a bit of information before I start. I want to be clear, Ms. Bettencourt, this could get ugly. I mean, perhaps you should remember the man you loved rather than--"

She stopped him short with a raised hand and gazed from behind the black veil. She was really studying him, and he had no idea what she saw. At one time he was the good guy. Now? Not so much. He had blood on his hands. Not just Laraunt's and Johnson's, but others as well. Whatever she saw she liked, because she broke her silent discrimination and said, "I'll take my chances." She stood. "You find out about the static."

They set up a meeting at her house for the following morning. He wanted to see where and how they had lived. Maybe have a cup of coffee with the widow. See some photos, books, and clothes. Get a feel for who he'd been in life. Maybe pick up a vibe. He suspected tension in their relationship. Maybe some shenanigans.

4a

The buzzing alarm roused Jimmie about half past six. He sat up on the old leather couch and looked around the cluttered space. He pushed up to his feet and walked to the sink in the corner where he splashed cold water on his face and brushed his teeth. Digging through a stack of clothes on a lone dining chair, he found a pair of faded jeans and a long sleeve shirt. He put them on along with a pair of hiking boots then slid on the shoulder holster.

He was supposed to meet the widow about 9 a.m. for coffee and a chat. That gave him enough time to check out her and Mr. Bettencourt.

Sitting at his desk, Jimmie brought the computer to life with a swipe of his finger. In the search box, he plugged in J.B. Speed and James Bettencourt and voila. There he was. A distinguished looking man whose salt and pepper hair was neatly combed with a tasteful wave. He wore a tweed sports jacket with a solid tan scarf and smiled gently.

Clicking on the link, Jimmie arrived at a page dedicated to the museum's recent renovation and expansion. It was scheduled to reopen in a couple days, and James Bettencourt had secured several key pieces of the expanded collection. Seems he had swooped into New Orleans after hurricane Katrina and used his family connections and university money to procure, among other things, a fine collection of dolls, gri-gris, and other spooky bric-a-brac.

His search on Elaine revealed a surprise. She had been a beauty queen and no slouch at that. Miss Kentucky and runner up for Miss America.

The photo online showed a thin-necked, full-cheeked beauty with high cheekbones, icy blue eyes, and a sugary, round-toothed smile that he'd seen nothing of. Long black hair hung in gracefully-swirling curls down past her collar bones to pile up on her full breasts.

She was the perfect balance of round and straight, soft and firm. An extraordinary beauty. This was a case of beauty and the geek. James Bettencourt had plenty to live for unless she'd done him wrong or he'd messed things up. Lots of ways to screw up a relationship. He wondered how they got together in the first place. He'd ask the princess herself.

He went out the back and walked to his BMW: a gift from Constance Murphy. Standing for a moment, He stared into its shiny black surfaces then stepped in, fired it up, and pulled around to the front of his office. It was still early. The sun had just begun to light up Berry Boulevard. He sat for a moment to watch the headlights move left and right then, when all was clear, he turned left and drove toward Taylor Boulevard.

When Jimmie reached Taylor, he turned left and headed toward Churchill Downs. Reaching Central, he turned right and saw the jumble of buildings that constitute Churchill Downs. In the midst of the dark rectangles he saw the silhouettes of the twin spires and felt a little hometown Derby pride.

He turned right on Fourth Street, pulled in next to Wagner's Café across from the backside entrance to the track, and parked on the side of the wide gravel drive. Walking along the building toward

Fourth, he noticed a graffiti artist's tag. A simple portrait of a rather worried fellow.

Walking around the corner, he stepped from the crackling gravel onto the sidewalk covered by two steel plates. Makeshift manhole covers. Portals to Louisville's underground world of pipes and tunnels. He'd enter that soon enough.

He pushed through the door into the front dining room. It was a makeshift restaurant with a jumble of kitchen equipment sitting along the side wall. A long Formica-topped counter, tables, and a dishwashing station made up the dining area.

The place was packed with an eclectic mix of people, mostly grimy track workers but also clean horse owners and spiffy media types. No room at the counter, but there was one open table. Right in front of the door. Jimmie sat, and straight away the waitress walked up. She was a head-tilting gum chewer and she liked to click the end of her pen. She took his order for eggs and biscuits with gravy then rushed off behind the counter.

He tuned his ears for track gossip and soon enough heard a couple track hands talking about there being "something in the air lately." Something that made the horses uneasy, fidgety, unpredictable. They considered astrological causes. "Maybe it's the position of Venus relative to Earth." They laughed but reaffirmed their observations. "Somethin's goin' on."

"Yessir."

As that conversation faded, Jimmie heard the sizzling of ham steaks on the flat-top grill, smelled the tangy scent, and looked around the place. Black and white horse photos hanging everywhere. Hand-painted signs from the fifties. Simple. Cartoonish. Commercial. He watched a couple servers juke around the two square columns that stood in the passage between rows of tables. Then his waitress came around the end of the counter with his food. Two eggs over easy and a biscuit smothered with sausage gravy.

5a

After breakfast, Jimmie took Third Street toward the University of Louisville. Just as he could make out the Confederate monument in the distance, he turned right on Eastern Parkway. It was tree-lined and a bit hilly. On each side stood homes ranging from huge two-hundred-year-old Victorians to small contemporary cubes. It was all there along Eastern Parkway and its cross streets that led into exclusive enclaves of fairytale cottages or rundown shotgun houses or grimy industrial areas or cemeteries. And at the end was the roundabout with a statue of Daniel Boone in the center.

He veered right and went up Cherokee Road. The woods of Cherokee Park stood on the left and high-dollar homes on the right. Ms. Bettencourt had a big hilltop place not far from the roundabout.

He pulled to the side of the road and got himself together. He wanted to get a feel for James. Maybe check the area for a source of static. Construction work. Electrical transformers. Whatever. He was wide open to possibilities. One thing was certain: The widow wanted answers. One thing was likely: She had money to pay him well.

Jimmie stepped from his Beemer and walked up the stone-lined walkway. It was a steep and difficult approach, and he struggled but made it to the large front porch lined with scalloped columns topped with ornate capitols. He rang the bell and leaned against one of the columns while he caught his breath. Looking through the leaded glass of the front door he saw the foyer: a vacant stage awaiting her arrival. After a few minutes, she appeared. Dressed again in black but without the veil, she walked to the door and opened it.

"Jimmie." She gestured gracefully for him to enter.

He looked at her face: a perfect oval of flawless skin. The center of which was her small nose.

"Please come in." She took his hand and led him into a formal living room where she bid him sit. When he did, she poured two cups of coffee from a silver pot. "Cream and sugar?" She smiled a round-toothed smile, and he melted. She was that beautiful. Like an angel. Like a demon. Like a dream.

Looking at her sitting so elegantly in the chair Jimmie fell silent. Just looked at her. In awe of her beauty and presence, his mind went blank, and he felt only the desire for her. Cellular lust. Bestial longing.

"Cream and sugar?" He watched her lips move, and a tingle ran along his spine. It flowed through his body in waves of erotic energy.

"Jimmie?"

"Sure." He took his coffee black but couldn't say no to her or her sparkling eyes or her smooth lips or small ears.

After stirring his coffee, she sat in an off-white wingback chair and crossed her legs. He noticed her black, patent-leather pumps and calves sheathed in shiny black hose. His body pulsed with the sensations of lust, and he had to cut them off in a hurry. "Nice weather," he blurted.

She looked at him, tilted her head slightly, and smiled. "Yes." Her voice was whisper soft. "It is."

Jimmie wasn't prepared for the intensity of her sexual appeal. Seeing her face clearly for the first time had really thrown him off his game. Feeling her eyes on me, he managed to sip his coffee without spilling any on himself. Now what was he saying? Oh yeah. "Cold last night. Warm and sunny today."

"March in the Ohio Valley." She was letting him off the hook. Now he could get down to business.

"What can you tell me about him?" He blinked. "Mr. Bettencourt."

"He hadn't been himself." She leaned forward to set her cup on its saucer. "For several months. He just talked about what a horrible person he was. How he'd hurt so many people. His mother and father. Women. Especially women. How he'd treated them so badly all his life. Like they were beneath him. He seemed to want to make it up to me. He took me out to dinner but confessed that he imagined stabbing me in the neck with the steak knife."

Jimmie couldn't quite comprehend what she was telling him. Was James Bettencourt crazy? He must have been.

"Is that all men? Tell me Jimmie, do all men feel like that?"

Her gaze penetrated his soul, and he knew she could see his desire. He imagined wallowing between her legs, listening to her moan while he worked away to take them to a new plane of consciousness. From the moment he'd seen her he'd wanted her. She could see that, but he could see into her soul as well. She needed him. She needed his adoration and desire. She needed his longing and ultimate satisfaction. They were made for each other.

He felt her attractive force grow stronger. It pulled him into her. His gaze penetrated her, and he saw her swirling aura. Drifted toward it. But there was something else. Something black and opaque. Impenetrable. Something scary. He pulled back from her. Withdrew. Had to get back on track.

"Any drugs?" Jimmie cleared his throat. "Did he do drugs?"

"He smoked some pot. Dropped acid back in the day."

He was thinking flashbacks as he looked around the room and saw a framed photo of the Bettencourts. A wedding photo. Mr. and Mrs. smiling and happy as she settled into his embrace. "How'd y'all meet?"

"After college. I did an internship at the museum. We met there and became friends. One thing led to another." She tilted her head to the side. "We fell in love."

"And what did you study in school?"

"Art History." She smiled. "Earned my Master's."

"Will you show me his study?"

"Certainly." She stood. "This way."

Following her up a flight of curving stairs, he could make out her beauty queen figure. Thin waist. Round hips and bottom with fabric draping on it. And, beneath that, the thing that sane men seek. He caught her scent. The subtle aroma of rose water that tingled as it travelled through him and stirred desire even deeper within his body.

She must have felt his gaze on her, because she turned to catch him looking, and a smile played across her face.

She was playing with him. Had him in the palm of her hand. He wanted her, and she knew it. He wanted to curl up next to her, and she knew it. But he knew she needed it as much as he did. She needed him to take her at the top of the stairs. She needed him to give her release. He imagined her moans echoing through the high-ceilinged rooms as the pent up energy broke from her.

Jesus, she had him twisted. He ached with longing for her but had to wait. Business before pleasure and all that. He took a deep breath and let it pass in a sudden burst. His tension faded, and he looked about to see they were standing at a door.

"Here it is." She gestured toward the entrance. "This is where I found him." She walked past him back down the hall. "I'll be downstairs if you need me."

Jimmie stood for a moment to reorient himself. Had to get his mind back on the case. Static and suicide. That's why he was standing outside the study of Mr. James Bettencourt. Static and suicide. Didn't make a damn bit of sense. He rubbed his cheek and then took the cool brass handle in his hand. It turned smoothly, and he swung the door open. The air, pungent with the aroma of cleaners, stirred for the first time in the week since the cleaning crew had finished their work, and the widow had closed the room.

Looking into the room, Jimmie saw a large window with a nice view of the wooded park across the road. His desk faced the window. It was an old oak piece with a leather chair. Along both walls to either side of the window, floor to ceiling bookshelves held countless volumes.

He stepped in and straight away noticed to his left a large piece of art over the fireplace mantle. It was a construction made with what looked to be rib bones from some large animal. They were laid out in a grid. Kind of a tic-tac-toe arrangement. Here and there were placed shiny chunks of bone. Polished pieces of skull. He pulled out his phone and took a picture. Then he walked to the desk. Opening the top drawer, He caught the scent of marijuana. Rummaging through it he found no weed. No papers or lighter. He did find a Waterman fountain pen. Probably the one he used to write his suicide note. At the back of the drawer, among paperclips and loose staples, he found a lady's ring: rose gold with an oval onyx inlaid with an ornate K. It was obviously out of place. Elaine's or otherwise, it wouldn't be missed, so he slipped it into his pocket.

Jimmie looked through the other drawers but found only a memory card, which he also pocketed. Other than that, nothing special. No unpaid bills. No indications of marital distress. He stood for a moment and listened closely but heard only the occasional passing of a car below. Peering through the window He saw no signs of recent roadwork or other construction. There were no cell towers visible. No probable or even possible source of "static." But the road sounds. Those may have been enough to set him off if he were having a flashback. Still that didn't explain everything. The long term depression, guilt, and violent impulses.

Jimmie checked out the bookshelves. More hocus pocus stuff. Treatise on Egyptian magic and

Voodoo and Reiki. Mummies and pyramids and burial mounds. Books by Aldous Huxley, Ken Casey, Alistair Crowley, and Carlos Castaneda. He'd seen enough. James was into beautiful women and drugs and the occult. At least they had common interests.

Back downstairs, Jimmie found the widow finishing her coffee. He had a few questions for her.

"His phone. Can I see it?"

She turned to leave, and Jimmie shifted his eyes to her bottom. She was a fine woman. Solid but soft. Graceful. He watched her walk into the kitchen and felt his heart palpitate. Visions of her rose in his mind. Ms. Bettencourt leaning on J.B.'s desk. Presenting herself in shiny black panties.

"Here it is."

He blinked the vision from his mind, looked at her, and smiled.

Handing him the phone, she smiled back.

"Can I take it with me?"

"Sure."

He turned for the door but stopped. "One more thing."

"Yes."

"The bones on the wall of his office?"

"It's a veve."

"A veve?"

"A voodoo design used to invoke a god."

"Of course." He chuckled. "Which one?"

She licked her lips. "I'm not sure."

6a

Leaving Ms. Bettencourt's Jimmie pulled a U-turn to head back toward the roundabout and Eastern Parkway. Immediately he noticed a tan van parked on the left. Not a work van. A people hauler with three or four rows of seats and lots of windows. When Jimmie passed it he saw a man behind the steering wheel look away. Not like he was looking at or for something. Just avoiding eye contact. He knew then, he had a tail.

He'd have to see how serious he was, so he veered right at the statue of Daniel Boone and went into the park where he slowed for the van to catch up. Jimmie wanted to have a bit of fun, so he cruised along for a while enjoying the scenery and the sensations of a morning drive along the wooded hills.

The air was cool, and the sun was still low in the sky, but the scene had a brightness he hadn't seen for a few months. From time to time as Jimmie topped a hill or came around a curve, the sun, shining white in the blue-grey sky, forced him to look away. He'd shift his gaze to the road or the fields where daffodils had sprouted from the moist earth or the hillside, covered with the bare forms of oaks and a few still-green pines.

Here and there he crossed or rode along Beargrass Creek, flowing slowly around stones and reflecting the forests beyond. As Jimmie enjoyed himself, he wondered what his friend was doing behind him. Was he growing furious about his flippancy? Banging his steering wheel at his cheekiness? He didn't bother glancing back.

Jimmie knew he was there. The detective knew when he slowed to a crawl his tail would have to choose between passing him and stopping, and Jimmie knew he'd chose to stop. When he did the van came up close and Jimmie caught a glimpse of the driver's face in the rear-view. Seemed familiar. Black hair slicked across his head. Clean-shaven. Square-jawed. Suit coat. He was every televangelist, con man, swindler, and used-car salesman he'd ever seen.

He'd peeped him and let him know the game was on. That's when Jimmie punched the gas to rush up the hill. His stomach tingled from sudden acceleration and the blood rushed from his face as the Beemer sped toward and over the peak. Behind him, his new friend had just begun his smoky pursuit.

The van chuffed along, but Jimmie carried more speed through the curves and accelerated faster in the straightaways. It took the detective just a minute of hard driving to shake his tail.

7a

Back at his office Jimmie sat down to go through Mr. Bettencourt's phone. He had hoped to find photos of the widow. Some nice shots of her in silk would have been perfect, but there were none. She was too tasteful for that sort of thing. Instead, he found a message thread from December of the previous year. The messages with someone identified as "X" referred to the exchange of "it" for "the money" to take place at the "Southwest campus." Jimmie jotted the number in his spiral notebook and continued snooping.

The message thread between Mr. and Mrs. B. displayed lots of affection. Plenty of pet names and references to their activities. Seems things had been pretty good up to a point: January of this year. That's when things went sour. Very few messages and the first mention of "static."

The phone was lots of help, but the memory card really opened his eyes. He exchanged it for the one in James Bettencourt's phone, restarted the device, and thumbed through a series of black and white close-ups of something that resembled the skin of a raisin. Each revealed a distinctly different underlying form that ranged from flat to slightly arcing to fully-curved. The form was complex, and he had no idea what it was until he saw the first image of a human hand. Blood rushed to his face as astonishment overcame him. Jimmie looked again at the photo to see the shiny jut of wrist bones, gnarled knuckles, and the thin fingers of two hands in the pose of a corpse. That was it. The corpse from the suicide note.

Jimmie swiped the screen until he saw a full image. It showed the shriveled corpse of a man. Skin shining like polished leather but wrinkled except the face, where it pulled tight over the skull so that the cheek and brow bones stood out prominently. The lips parted to reveal the lighter teeth and a black space where one was missing.

Astonished, he felt his heart pound out some crazy poly-rhythmic beat as sweat beaded up on his forehead. Jesus Christ all mighty this was a mummy. Not wrapped up Egyptian style but naked and staring with glass eyes. James Bettencourt was not raving when he mentioned the corpse. He was dirty. He'd been dealing artifacts on the black market. It was time to look again at the suicide note.

He pulled it from the top drawer of his desk and read it again. This time with conviction that it was not the raving of a tripped out art geek but the truth.

Dearest Elaine,

I can't take it anymore. This damned static. It hisses like channel zero. Squeals like short wave radio. It cuts through me like an x-ray and growls like a robotic dog digging through my mind. It uncovers my worst memories. Like the corpse. Its taut face haunts me. I shouldn't have given it to them. No matter how much they offered. Now look at me. A victim of my own greed. I knew what they would do. I knew the fanatics would try to kill all us

wayward souls. I just didn't believe it
would work, but this pistol is proof. This
pistol and this damned noise. Crackling
static. Fucking nonsense and guilt drive
me to my death.

    J.B.

He'd found proof of the corpse. No sign of static that he was aware of. Who were the fanatics and how were they trying to kill the "wayward souls"?

He grabbed his phone and dialed the number associated with "X." It rang a few times then a lady answered, "Southern Christian Church."

Things were coming together quickly.

Jimmie decided to head down to the church the next morning.

8a

That evening, Jimmie smoked weed in the back room of his office and settled back on the old leather couch to recall a recent evening when he'd held Peaches' small body from behind. They'd snuggled on the couch, and he'd wrapped her in his arms. Pressed warm against her. She was skinny. Almost bony. And he thought of healing her. He ran a hand smoothly along her thin arm and felt the muscles of her shoulder soften to his touch. She let out a gentle breath and settled into his embrace.

Jimmie nestled his face into her hair to nibble her earlobe. When he did, she rolled her face toward his, and they kissed long and soft. Gently, he licked her lips and slid his hand up to caress her breast. She had picked up some weight since she'd been coming around. He could feel it there in his hand.

Jimmie's enjoyment was interrupted when someone knocked on his door. He thought it may be her, but she didn't knock anymore and that would become a problem. The sudden rapping startled him, and Jimmie turned to see, in the dim light of his room, an envelope slide beneath the door. It scuffed across the tile floor then came to rest several feet from the black door. The detective looked at it, this anonymous invasion of his solitude, while the unknown person who'd delivered it beat a hasty retreat.

Jimmie was too caught up in the moment to think or act. He watched it slide and rotate across the floor in the dim light from his lamp. Then he walked to it, bent, and picked it up to read his name in blue ink: Waterman Mysterious Blue. The same color James Bettencourt had used.

226

The envelope was the size of a typical greeting card, and someone had taken the trouble to seal it. Jimmie tore off the end and slid out a picture, then walked to the lamp and held the photo in the light. It showed a landscape scene: a hillside with a bare tree in the foreground. Beneath the tree, brown leaves lay in a circle on the green grass that extended up the hill where a few more dormant trees stood. Next to the trees, standing out in bright red on the hilltop, a huge steel sculpture captured his attention. It was a multifaceted assemblage of planes and girders that challenged the tree for hilltop dominance.

The detective could appreciate the artistry of the photograph and the scene, but what most interested him was the figure the sculpture presented against the light grey sky. It was the reason someone had slipped him the photo. It was an ornate K. Seemed he was being led by the nose, but by who? The widow had his vote.

Morning light made its way into the back room of his office and woke him slowly. Jimmie dressed, made a pot of coffee, and then went to his computer to investigate the red K. A quick image search on "outdoor sculpture" yielded too many results to be useful. He tried "sculpture park" and straight away found the piece. It was called "Abracadabra" and was in Pyramid Hill Sculpture Park in Hamilton, Ohio, just north of Cincinnati.

At his fingertips, Jimmie had all the details: Dates. Artist. Location. But what if whoever had slipped the picture under his door was trying not so much to point out the sculpture but to lead him to that exact spot. Perhaps there was something important to either side or a scent in the air. The internet would not do. It was time for a road trip. First he'd swing by the church to check it out.

He got in his car and navigated through the decrepit lot to pull onto Berry Boulevard. Passing coin laundries and tattoo parlors, he came to the intersection with Manslick Road where he stopped for a red light. The Derby City Lounge sat on the opposite corner. Peaches had worked there for a while before starting at the Fog Light. That's where her problems with drugs began.

That intersection was the epicenter of Peaches' life. She lived around the corner just past the White Castle and worked at the Fog Light Club. Didn't have or need a car. Did her laundry and bought her food on Berry. That neighborhood was all she knew. Grew up there. On Lentz Avenue. Sometimes Jimmie wondered if it bothered her that her neighbors and the people she'd grown up with had seen her naked. Guess not.

He drove past Peaches' apartment complex on the right. It was a two-story block job with exposed walkways. Continuing, Jimmie drove down Manslick Road past a seemingly endless array of churches and liquor stores and gas stations and cemeteries. Over hills and through curves past Gagel and Palatka and Blanton. All the while, Jimmie thought of doe-eyed Peaches. What was he going to do with her? They'd become a bit of a couple. Somehow.

It started a few days after Mary's funeral. He'd stopped in the Fog Light for a bite and saw her there in the black and purple and chrome environment. It may have been our grief or the insistent rhythm of the music or the influence of Haley's Comet somewhere far off in the galaxy that urged him to hold her a little extra when she put her skeletal hand on his shoulder and laid her withered cheek on his chest.

That night she knocked on his back door and when he open it, she kinda looked down and asked to come in. When he let her in, she said she'd heard about Randall Johnson and without saying anything more she loosened the tie on his terrycloth robe and thanked him as she saw fit.

That's how they got started. There would have been no problem had it stopped there, but she kept coming to his door, letting herself in to lay with him in the old leather couch and do the things that men and women do. He didn't mind the sex but knew she was falling in love. That was the problem. Jimmie wasn't ready for love again. Not so soon after Mary's death.

Then he came to the church on the left in the middle of a strong right hand turn. It was a large building with a hunter green roof. It sat in front of a high, wooded hillside so that the white cross atop the peak of the roof stood out against the bare trees.

The entrance was blocked by a metal gate secured with a chain and padlock. There was nothing special about the place besides its somewhat secluded location. Pretty good place to exchange possession of a corpse. Round back perhaps. Lots of privacy there. But other than that. Why there in particular? Seemed the place was shut off when there were no services. The gate would have been closed. "X" must have had a key. Must have been associated with the church. So what would such a person want with a mummy unless it was a religious relic?

While the detective pondered this, the tan van that had followed him through Cherokee Park pulled to a hard stop behind his Beemer. A jolt of energy passed through his body, and he popped open his door. Craning his neck to look back, Jimmie saw the overly-groomed man step from the van and straighten his suit coat. Jimmie swung his legs out and was beginning to stand when he heard the slide and snap of the man's extending baton.

Jimmie stood just in time to take a blow across the bridge of his nose. The impact jarred his head and made him stumble. Pain rushed through his face, and tears flowed from his eyes to blur his vision. He tried to wipe them away with one hand while holding the other out in defense but still couldn't see. Jimmie heard the man's shoes scuff the pavement and shifted his defensive hand to take the second blow. The metal bar struck the pinkie-side wrist bone to produce a white-hot explosion of pain. Jimmie pulled the hand back instinctively and held it for a second.

The detective's eyes were clearing and he saw the man's sneering face: clean-shaven and shiny-smooth. The man stepped to his right, and Jimmie followed suit. Extending his left hand again in defense, the detective pulled his Smith and Wesson from its shoulder holster with his right. Jimmie flashed it low by his side. The man's eyes darted to it, and his face froze for an instant, but he continued looking for an opening to attack.

"Slow down, buddy." We continued circling. "I don't wanna blast ya." He licked his lips to taste blood. "But I will."

"What say we get back in our cars and drive away?" Jimmie wiped the last of the tears from his eyes. "Call this a draw."

The man paused and licked his lips. A far off expression came over his face, and Jimmie waited for him to return. When he did, he lowered his weapon and laughed. "The Reverend will have his way with you." He turned and walked back to his van, laughing the whole way.

Jimmie didn't know what that was all about. For sure, someone was very interested in his activities. But who? The widow or "X" perhaps? Or "The Reverend?" He needed a scorecard.

He'd had enough for the day, so he headed back toward his office, shivering with adrenaline and checking his rearview the whole way. Turning right on Berry, Jimmie relaxed a little. This was home. He felt safe there where he knew every pothole and blind corner. Every oil stain and patch of gravel. Every troubled boy and endangered girl.

Jimmie pulled into the Fog Light parking lot and drove behind his office. Blood had coagulated in his nostrils and was oozing down his throat, so he breathed through his mouth, and each breath had the foul taste of old pennies. Favoring his left arm, he opened the car door with his right and spit a thick stream of blood onto the rough asphalt. When he did, pressure built in his sinuses, and pain swelled so that he felt like the top of his head would explode. Jimmie struggled out and made his way to the black metal door. For once, he was glad the lock on the door didn't work, because he wouldn't have been able to fit a key into it. Couldn't see straight with the tears blurring his vision.

Pushing the door open, Jimmie entered the darkness of his back room, and a rush of relief softened his tense body. He drew a deep breath and exhaled. That's when the pain really came on strong to surge through his face and arm with every beat of his heart. Jimmie wished for some Oxi but knew he'd have to make do with Aspirin. He wasn't getting back on that tormenting death ride.

Jimmie went to the sink and started some cold water. Filling his palms, he gently rinsed his nose. A sharp sting revealed a gash through the skin across the bone. It bled into the cold water, flowed down the sides of his nose and into his mustache and beard. Bloody water dripped from the tip of his nose and the hairs of his beard into the white porcelain sink mounted to the wall. The water stung the cut, but he needed to reduce the swelling, so he kept it running. After a while the water ran clear, and he dared to look at himself in the small rectangular mirror above the sink. Two black eyes, badly swollen. Nose with still-trickling cut surrounded by purple skin. His shirt was ruined with blood. The whole chest of it soaked. He checked his wrist. There was a knot on the bone. Jimmie coughed, spit blood into the sink, and then rinsed his mouth. He soaked a wash cloth with rubbing alcohol and pressed it against the cut. That was the worst pain of all. A dizzying, strobe-lit affair that made him grimace and clench his teeth until his jaws ached with tension. After that bit of torture, Jimmie went over to his couch to rest.

Settling into the cushions, he soon fell asleep. That's when the dream came to him. It was a high-resolution dream. More like a movie in its clarity and realism. It was as though he'd suddenly become a receiver tuned to some strange transmission, featuring a cloaked skeleton, a dark edifice, and a soundtrack of barely-audible, hissing static.

Jimmie woke slowly to find Peaches naked by his side. She had her right cheek on his bare chest and was stroking his beard with the fingertips of her left hand. He managed a slight smile as he looked into her eyes.

"Poor baby." She gave him a little kiss. "Can I make it better for you?" he felt her other hand down below, just barely fondling him so that he slowly grew aroused. Then a rush of static cut through him, made him jolt with tension.

Peaches raised her head and looked into his eyes. "Easy, baby." She smiled. "It's me. Your peachy girl." She kissed him gently and he felt the delicious sensation followed by a second shock of static, spreading through his body like fever chills. All the same, she had him aroused, and he wanted to make love, but every time Jimmie thought of joining with her or enjoying her touches the hissing static cut through his mind and body.

"So this is the static."

"What's that, sweetie?" She whispered into his ear, "Static?"

He reached up to stroke her side, felt the row of ribs and jutting hip bone. A pain began growing at the base of his skull as she climbed on top of him, parted the way for him to enter, and then started.

All the while, Jimmie's pain grew steadily along with the increasing volume of the static. He managed to finish, and that's when he heard for the first time since his boyhood the big, bone-rattling, baritone pronounce its favorite phrase: "Thou shalt not."

Peaches continued thrusting and moaning, and a shock of revulsion came over Jimmie. He looked wide-eyed upon her in the midst of her passion. She was disgusting, he thought. Her face contorted with animal lust. Her bony body gyrating in a grotesque display of wantonness.

Jimmie thrust her off of him with his left hand, and she fell to the linoleum floor.

Sprawled out angular like a fallen tree, she looked up at him. "What's wrong, baby?"

"Get your clothes. Get out."

"What?" Confusion marked her voice. "Don't you want me?"

"You disgust me."

Tears came to her big eyes, and she lowered her head as she gathered her clothes. She walked to the back door, cracked it just a little so that a swath of light flowed into the dark room. His head hurt from the beating and the static, and he could hardly bare to look at her so soiled and disgusting. She stood for a moment and looked back.

"Go on," he grunted, "whore."

Jimmie heard her break as she passed through the door into the parking lot beyond. Then he lay in the bright shaft of the afternoon sun passing through the open door.

10a

Pulling onto the Watterson, Jimmie hoped the headache would pass, and by the time he crossed beneath 64 it had lessoned to a sharp pain at the base of his skull. When he passed Gene Snyder Expressway on 71 it had nearly faded away.

Just as he passed the Crestwood exit he heard something interesting on the radio. The announcer said, "The CDC has declared the recent spate of suicides in the Louisville area an epidemic." She continued to say there had been over 50 suicides in the past three months, and authorities were investigating the cause. They weren't the only ones. He wondered if they too were hot on the trail of the red K and laughed. Not likely.

Around Carrolton, the signal began to cut out, so he turned off the radio and enjoyed the drive. The sun shined, his BMW cruised along, and he felt as though he'd just escaped a rusty cage. Somehow – he couldn't explain it – he felt an oppressive weight fall from him. Jimmie breathed more freely and even hummed a tune as he passed the Florence water tower.

Beginning the descent toward Covington, he saw Cincinnati across the river. Lots of tall, bright buildings. Glass and steel towers piled against one another in a dense display of urbanity. He crossed the bridge and continued on 75 north until he reached Hamilton about a half hour later.

Cruising down Erie Boulevard, he saw railroad tracks on the right and a brown stucco building with large signs advertising Mountain Dew and Pepsi. This was Hyde's Restaurant. He pulled into the lot and

236

parked. Stepping from the Beemer, he stretched his legs and rolled his shoulders.

Passing through the entrance into the dining area, Jimmie smelled toast and thought of hot chocolate. Perhaps he'd get a cup. Dip his toast into it. He looked around. The place was packed. It was Sunday morning, and everyone wanted breakfast and pie. Old ladies with puffed up hair and floral print blouses. Old men with bald spots and tissue-thin skin. He walked along the cracked but clean linoleum tile floor. Squares of various light tans and greys with no discernable pattern. The dining hall was large and open with many rectangular tables and bench seats.

He found an open table near the servers' station, slid into the orange-brown bench, and looked around the place. Large square windows with a view of Erie Boulevard and the railroad tracks beyond. Square ceiling tiles. A few black and white photos. Old military images. A few color photos of local sports teams. A poster of Elvis. A wooden plaque that spelled out JESUS. Just to the left, about ten feet away, he spotted a lovely young lady. Long blond hair, a little wavy, and a beautiful face that showed keen interest in her breakfast companion: a young man seated with his back to the detective.

Jimmie flinched slightly when his waitress touched his shoulder. She was a middle-aged veteran server. Thin, fast-moving, efficient, and kind. He ordered coffee, a veggie omelet with potatoes, toast, and a slice of banana meringue pie.

Watching her write the order on a small pad, he noticed her rose tattoo. It covered half the length of her forearm and was faded, smeared, almost undecipherable. He wondered who she had loved and if their love had faded and blurred like her tattoo. She noticed him looking and smiled, said she'd get his order in straight away and be right back with his coffee.

While Jimmie waited, he studied the blonde. Thin body with a roundish face. A few rips in her faded blue jeans. She was focused on her companion, but from time to time their eyes met, and he looked away.

His food arrived. Rich yellow omelet oozing orange cheddar cheese, red tomatoes, and green peppers. Diced boiled potatoes. Two slices of buttered toast.

He dug in and quickly finished the meal. Then came the banana meringue pie. A four-inch-high wedge of fluffy meringue, creamy pudding with chunks of banana and a dense but flaky crust. It was scrumptious but a bit too sweet. He looked over to the blonde. She and her man were still talking. Just then a train passed by. He watched the cars move from right to left. Box cars and tanks clanged and rattled, and a piece of graffiti on one of them caught his attention. A simple piece in white that read "I MISS YOU."

Jimmie thought of Mary lying dead on the bed in the Hyatt. A figure in black across the white sheet. He thought of Francesca lying dead in his arms. A heavy weight pulling him down. He thought of Peaches. A broken girl crying on his floor.

Driving down Pyramid Hill Boulevard, Jimmie saw on his right the entrance to the sculpture park. Pulling in, he saw that the road passed through a huge red sculpture comprised of long, crisscrossing beams. They straddled the passage and resembled a pile of needles or twigs leaning against one another in a moment of uneasy stasis. A flash of fear passed through him, and his heart skipped a beat.

This promised to be an excellent trip, so he pulled out a joint to heighten the experience. The road was empty and the forest setting gave him enough privacy to take a few hits then turn his attention to the red thing before him. The beams were falling. Certainly, given the insistence of gravity and time, they would fall. But when? Could he make it through before they fell? Trapped him in his car. Crushed him in a bloody mess. That was the question of the moment. It was a challenge, and he had to want what was beyond that portal enough to risk everything.

Jimmie wanted to know about "Abracadabra," who had sent him there, and why. He wanted to know bad enough to risk passing through that precarious tangle of red beams, so he took his foot from the brake, hesitated for a moment, and then pressed gently on the gas. The car crept forward and the red thing rose up through the view in his windshield. Slowly, he approached the passage and just as he came directly below the mass of red beams, hope rose to mingle with fear, and a burst of energy swept through his body. He stepped hard on the gas pedal. The car shot forward with the squeal of tires, and, in an instant, he was free and clear of the possibility of disaster.

The detective slowed to a stop and exhaled with relief. Tension faded from his neck, his cheeks went loose, and he shook his head in amazement. This was going to be a great trip. He sat and breathed for a minute, let the excitement fade from his body until he felt the steady beat of his heart.

Jimmie started up the hill to the visitor's center. It was a steep ascent, but he didn't let himself get carried away with fear. He simply clung to the hope that he'd arrive safely. When he did, he rented a cart and met the facility manager, Ray Harmon: a thin, well-dressed man with dark hair slickly combed to the side.

They shook hands, and Jimmie let him know why he was there.

"Drove all the way from Louisville to see Abracadabra."

"That's a long trip." He nodded with a serious expression.

"Yeah."

"You a fan of Liberman?"

Jimmie must have given him a puzzled look, because he elaborated. "The artist."

"Oh, yeah." He blinked. "This piece in particular."

"A lot of people travel here from around the world to see it." He smiled. "How'd you discover it?"

"A friend thought I should see it."

"That's a good friend." He smiled. "What would you like to know about it?"

"I'm not sure. Just wanted to come here and experience it. From a particular spot." He pulled the photo from his pocket and showed him. He worried that he was being too weird but dismissed the thought.

"I know the spot. Just follow the gallery loop. You'll know when you get there." He smiled. "Be sure to listen to the rooster." Ray patted him on the shoulder and pointed him toward the door. Just as Jimmie was about to pass through the exit, Ray said, "By the way, the artist originally called it 'Abrahadabra.'"

"With an 'h'?" He licked his lips.

"Yes."

"I wonder why."

"Might make interesting research."

"Yeah." Jimmie turned and went through the door.

It was a dark grey noon. Clouds drooped in the sky, and a mist of rain fell as he crossed to the cart, took his seat, and started down the paved gallery loop. To his left he saw a rooster leaning back to give the wakeup call. He heard its cackling and perked up to look around and saw to his left on top of the hill the huge red sculpture. A little further down the path he saw a tall, rectangular stone with a slit cut through it. The artist had filled the slit with blue glass, and he was certain that at a particular time of day the sun would shine through the slit to point something out. The day was overcast and rainy, so there was no hope of experiencing that. Still, it let Jimmie know he was in a place where truths were revealed and mysteries solved. It was his kind of place.

Jimmie looked over his left shoulder to the red form on the hilltop and felt his curiosity grow. What was it? Why had he been directed there? What would he find at the top of that hill besides sheets of red steel?

After a fifteen minute drive on the gallery loop along the grassy hillside and wooded sections, Jimmie came to a decrepit stone structure on his left. He pulled over in front of it and immediately saw on the hilltop the big red K. He'd reached his destination. The spot at which he'd learn the reason he'd been summoned.

Looking to his right, he saw the remains of an original frontier stone building. On his left stood a large portal constructed from a weathered tree that had been cut into sections and arranged to form a doorway.

An old building, a portal, and "Abracadabra." his mind worked to find a connection. The building was but a husk, just a crumbling shell of creek stones beside which ran water from a spring. The doorway, being constructed of a minimally altered tree rather than lumber, hinted at the natural quality of the portal. He thought of death as the natural passage from one realm to another. "Abracadabra" was a stage magic term sort of like "Voila" or "Behold." Behold what? Death? The soul leaving the body, passing into another realm to leave the shell behind. And the spring? Eternal life, flowing from the very ground. Life and death and magic. Life and death and magic?

Jimmie stared up the hillside to the big red K. One could see it only from this point. From any other vantage it would present another aspect. The K would not be visible. His nighttime visitor, his secret informant had drawn him to this exact spot. Why?

Life and death and magic? He rubbed his hand on his cheek, felt it clammy cold. Just then, he saw something move at the base of the sculpture. A jolt of energy passed through him, and he set off toward the piece. Crossing the circle of fallen leaves beneath the large tree, Jimmie struggled along the steep hillside through the dry grass.

On the hilltop, he found a man dressed in black standing beneath the huge red form. He stood motionless for a second before speaking. "Hello, Jimmie."

His heart went crazy, and a strange sense of helplessness crept over him. "How'd you know my name?"

"I know a lot about you. Like who sent you here and why." He half smiled. "Do you know these things?"

"No."

"Consider it an invitation. Someone thinks you are worthy." The man in black looked at Jimmie. "I'm not so sure."

"Worthy of what?"

"Initiation."

"Initiation into what?"

"The secret and power of personal liberation. Access to the matrix of reality." He raised his brows.

Jimmie shook his head in disbelief.

"First you need my approval."

"I don't want it."

"Of course you do, Jimmie. You do, and she knows it."

"Elaine Bettencourt?"

"Yes. She feels your energy. She wants to join forces, but first you need my approval." He smiled. "Look at the sculpture. Tell me what you see."

Jimmie wandered beneath and between the red planes and beams, craned his neck to look through them to the grey sky cut into various shapes.

When he looked back toward the man in black he saw the man's form slowly dissolved and disappeared.

About the time Jimmie started picking up radio signals from Louisville, he heard something faint and hardly noticeable. Like the scent of a distant dog's rotting corpse drifting on a breeze, static crept into his awareness to cause his nerves to jangle and his mind to skitter this way and that.

Pent up energy sizzled slowly along the nerve fibers until even his bones ached with the desire to move. For several minutes he wriggled in the leather seat and tried desperately to distract himself. That continued until he reached exit 28 toward Bedford and a sudden recollection came to him.

He'd spent his middle school years in Bedford. His family had moved there to avoid the violence and chaos associated with forced bussing in Louisville. It had been a few years of exploring the woods, shooting guns and bows, and chewing tobacco. At the time of the memory, he'd been shooting bow for a while and could shoot targets with ease, but buck fever set in every time he drew back on an actual deer. Shaking all over, he'd empty his quiver shooting at a nearby deer but miss every shot. He'd never killed anything with an arrow. Never killed anything at all until one early evening in fall. He climbed a tree to about thirty feet and waited for a deer to pass on a trail or enter the opening below. He hadn't seen anything and was about to gather his gear and head home. Just then, something moved in the dry creek bed below. Looking closely, Jimmie saw a red fox and knew if he shot and killed that fox buck fever would be a thing of the past.

Steadying his nerves with a long breath, Jimmie drew the string back to his anchor point on the side of his jaw. Looking down on the fox, he saw his bushy tail twitch as he scampered about on the rocks of the creek bed. He adjusted his alignment in response to his movements and, just as his body began to stiffen with tension, he let the string slip from his fingers.

The arrow wobbled at first then straightened as it flew toward the unsuspecting fox. The razor broad head pierced his back and passed through his body. The fox yelped and swung his head around. Growling, he chewed on the arrow's shaft. After a second, his growls turned to whines and whimpers, and he settled down onto the cold stones.

That memory took him by surprise, and a shudder passed through him as his awareness returned to the highway. He'd seen it all as it happened, but the elation he'd felt at that moment had been replaced with something darker. All he felt was guilt and remorse for the killing.

Since that day, the day of his first kill, he'd taken many deer with well-placed shots and a few men as well. Each kill accompanied by a mixture of joy and regret. All but one. Michael Murphy had been different. There was neither joy nor regret.

Jimmie couldn't think about it then. Couldn't allow the memory to surface. His body tensed as a blast of static cut through him, and flashes of images and broken thoughts skittered around his mind. Recollections of distant memories: The time in middle school when he snapped a super-sized rubber band on the back of a boy's neck. The boy was sitting at the desk in front of Jimmie, and he really stretched it out. When he let the rubber strap go it zapped him hard and without warning.

35 years later, he heard the snap and saw the boy's big, moist eyes as he turned to look back. Tingling heat blazed through his body, rushed through his chest, and flushed his face. Guilt and shame poured over him, and he felt their taint. He'd shattered the boy's youthful innocence. Brought down the edifice of childhood with one thoughtless act. Had that been the boy's first experience of unmotivated violence? It was the first Jimmie had hurt someone. He'd hurt a lot of people since then. Insult and injury. Blood and broken bones. Jimmie had thought he was a hero. Perhaps he was wrong.

Jimmie had to stop this macabre parade of memories, so he turned to the meditation techniques he'd learned from Dao Tam, his Zen teacher from the monastery at Weise Landing. He'd always wanted to study and practice Zen but had no proper instruction until one day, when Francesca was still alive, he was riding his motorcycle toward Bedford and had a strong urge to explore the road to the side of the fruit market. Jimmie rode down it 'till it turned to rough gravel. Then he continued along the pitted and shifting way until he came to an opening where he saw a monumental statue of the Bodhisattva Avalokiteshvara.

Jimmie spent the next few years in intensive meditation practice. Occasionally, he stayed at the monastery and sat before the huge brass statue of Amitabha. Dao Tam led him in his devotion to the bodhisattva and encouraged him to take the bodhisattva vow to return until all beings were enlightened, which he did, and according to Dao Tam it wasn't his first time.

He'd lost his way after Francesca's murder. Became twisted up in a karmic knot with Doc Laraunt, until they dragged one another into that echo chamber at West Haden. But it didn't stop there. He'd been bound up with Peaches as well. Constance and Michael Murphy too. It was all playing out.

Taking a detour on his way back to Berry Boulevard, Jimmie rolled through Seneca Park, past Christian Academy, his alma mater, and on into Cherokee Park. He parked the Beemer and walked to Big Rock, where he'd celebrated his killing of Randal Johnson. Climbing onto the huge, square boulder, Jimmie took up the cross-legged posture and determined to accept whatever arose in his mind.

First came the little things. Easy things like the promises he'd broken and lies he'd told. Then, as he settled into deeper relaxation, came things harder to accept. Things that threatened his self-conception as the good guy. The extreme violence. One case in particular came to mind. Every detail as it happened.

***

It was a Friday afternoon like any other on Berry Boulevard. Grimy cars cruised back and forth in front of his office, young men wearing straight-billed ball caps leaned against the corners of buildings, and he sat at his desk to read the paper. Nothing but bad news. Baby killing. Riots. Terrorism. Not much he could do about all that. Then she walked in and offered him a mission. Seek and destroy.

Her name was Sally. A brunette with quivering chin, teary blue eyes, and not even the faintest trace of a smile. "Mr. Star." She blinked. "You've gotta help me."

Jimmie grasped her shoulder. It was small and delicate in his hand. "Have a seat. We'll talk about it."

She sat in the wooden chair across from his desk. He leaned on the edge of the desktop and studied her lifeless hair, drooping from her head and clinging close to her face, which was lovely by nature but neglected and damaged.

"It's a man." She slipped him a photograph. "Norman Lee."

The photo was blurry. It had obviously been taken on the down low. Showed a huge human-shaped lump with great bulging shoulders and shiny scalp.

She licked her cracked lips. "He beats me."

A rush of heat flowed through his face, and he closed his eyes for a moment to compose himself. "Y'all live together?"

"Nope. I hardly know him." She looked him nearly in the eyes. Didn't quite make full contact. "I'd seen him around a bar from time to time. Then one night several months ago, he started talking to me. One thing led to another, and we got together. Ever since, he comes over when he's drunk. He screws me then beats me up." She broke into tears, and he reached out to pat her shoulder.

"But that's not all." She studied her shoes for a moment then said, "He makes videos of it." Her shame was palpable. Her outrage complete. "Trades them with his friends."

His innards twisted into a square knot when he heard that. He licked his lips and swallowed hard. Looking at her small in the chair across from him, he wanted to scoop her up and hold her close, but this is a crazy game he plays. Encounter lotsa crossed wires in this business.

"You have proof?"

"Yeah. He keeps them on his phone."

"You got it?"

She shook her head.

"Can ya get it?"

"Not without some help."

"What kinda help?"

"I'll call you next time he's comin' over. I'll occupy him. You slip in and snatch his phone."

"Then we take it to the police?"

"Oh, no. Said he'd kill my little girl if I did." Shivering overtook her, as tears streamed from her eyes.

"Then what? What's the point?"

"I need you." She licked her lips and swallowed hard. "I need you to help me."

Jimmie knew what she wanted. Ever since he'd taken out Johnson and Laraunt, vigilante justice had been his specialty.

She looked him in the eyes, and he felt her desperation.

"I gotta see the videos first."

She blinked out two fat tears, and he knew he'd soon have blood on his hands.

She left her key and turned for the door. Just before taking the handle in her small hand, she turned back to him. "You're my only hope, Mr. Star."

He took a slow breath. "I know."

***

Early Saturday evening, Jimmie was thinking about Sally's case and the quickest route to her apartment in Okolona. It'd be a fifteen minute drive. Just as he had himself situated, she called to say Norman was drunk and headed her way. "Hurry." Her voice cracked. "He'll be here in half an hour. Please hurry. I'm so scared."

He felt for the key in his pocket, found it, and rushed out of his office. He jumped into his Beemer and tore off down Taylor Boulevard toward the expressway. On the roundabout onramp he felt his Smith and Wesson 38 Special heavy in his shoulder holster and hoped he wouldn't have to use it.

Just past the airport, Jimmie merged onto 65 south and gunned the engine. He wanted to beat him there. Watch him go in. Size him up.

A few minutes later he ran into traffic on Preston highway. As he cursed at the SUV in front of him, he kneaded the steering wheel and chewed his lips. Traffic crept beneath the light at Outer Loop, and just when the signal turned red, Jimmie shot through the intersection to arrive at his destination on the right. Pulling into the parking lot, Jimmie felt blood pulse in his neck. He found her building and parked. It'd only taken twenty minutes for him to get there, so he felt confident he'd beaten the bully. He had to settle himself, so Jimmie took a deep breath and let it slide out through barely-parted lips. He'd be no good to her if he was amped up. Gotta stay cool in this line of work.

Jimmie calmed himself and waited. When his heart had settled, he saw Norman pull up in a classic Impala with big shiny wheels. The car rocked when he stepped out. He was a slow-moving log of a man. Thick and brutish.

He walked to the door, knocked, and waited. When Sally didn't answer straight away he knocked again. This time she opened the door. He pushed past her, and she looked around for the detective. Their eyes met, and he gave her a little wave. She pressed her lips together as she closed the door.

For five desperate minutes, Jimmie rubbed his fingertips and checked his pistol for ammo and counted his breaths. Then he opened the door, stepped out, and headed for her unit with the key she'd given him in hand. He put his ear to the door but heard nothing, then he unsnapped the strap on his holster. Slipping the key into the lock, he felt heat spread through his chest and face. It was show time. He'd get the phone, check it out, and go from there.

Quietly, Jimmie turned the key and pushed the door open a bit. Peeking inside, he heard grunts from the back of the apartment, and his body tingled with the thrill of sneaking and snooping.

Jimmie stepped into the living room and searched the couch and end tables, then walked into the kitchen to check on the countertops. Not there. He crept down the hall past a small pink bedroom to her carnal chamber. The sounds of their sex filled the hall. It was no joyous song. Rather desperate and joyless. He stood in the doorway and peered around the corner to see Norman's big hairy back humped up like a loaf of bread. Red-faced, Sally met his gaze. Jimmie shrugged, and she flashed her eyes to the bedside table. There it was. His phone.

Jimmie motioned for her to keep him calm, and she held his head close to her and began to slowly stroke the hairy bulk of his back. The detective took a deep breath and stepped into the room.

Walking slowly along the long side of the squeaking bed, Jimmie saw his thrusting bulk and smelled him cheesy and gross. At the table, Jimmie looked down to see her suffering still and silent beneath him. Jimmie eased his hand out until he grasped the phone. Norman was getting pretty excited about then. Really going at it. By the time he'd slipped out of there and ducked into the little girl's room to check out the phone, he was done.

The phone had a pattern password, which Jimmie got right on the first try. Classic SS lightning bolt. About the time he found his photo gallery, the detective heard Norman exclaim, "Where the hell's my phone?"

He looked around for a non-lethal weapon. Nothing except stuffed animals on the neatly-made twin bed. Then Jimmie heard him toss over the bedside table.

"Dammit, bitch. Where is it?"

Jimmie's body tightened. His jaws clenched. He wanted to rush in there to shut him up, but the louse had done nothing but shout.

"What'd you do with it?"

Norman rushed down the hall past the pink room to the living room. While he ransacked the living room, Jimmie slipped into the closet and eased the door shut. In the darkness, among the frilly girl clothes, he riffled through the phone in search of the incriminating videos. Soon enough Jimmie found a few pictures of Sally with black eyes. His heart went wild when he saw them, and he started to feel confined in that closet. Sally was crying in the next room. He found a video of the man screwing her doggie style. Getting a bit rough. Knocking her around some. Nothing too extreme. Just when he thought he may have to slip through the window without addressing her concerns, Jimmie hit pay dirt. A video of him smacking her across a coffee table and choking her until she turned red.

"Gimme your phone." He yelled to Sally. "I'm gonna call it."

Jimmie's heart thumped as he fumbled through the screens for the ringtone volume control. In his desperation, he stuffed the phone under a pile of blankets just as the ringtone started. His body jolted, and his eyes sprang open, as the 80's style video game ringtone sang out. Muffled but audible, the ringtone would inevitably lead Norman to Jimmie's hiding place.

Sally tried to cover the ringtone with cries, and Jimmie heard a loud smack. That's when he formed his resolve. He had no choice. He'd seen the evidence, and the brute was going buck wild at the moment. The detective pulled his piece from his shoulder holster and waited for Norman to open the door.

"Jesus, Norman, what's the gun for." Sally warned Jimmie.

That damn ringtone droned on. It called Norman to Jimmie like an emergency beacon sending its signal through space to alert the mother ship. He would follow it. He would open the closet door, and a battle of reflexes would determine the survivor.

The detective crouched a bit in the increasingly hot closet. Sweat stung his eyes and dripped from his face. Kneading the pistol grip in his hand, Jimmie heard him lumber down the hall toward the pink room. Every fiber of his body coursed with fierce energy and lethal intention. All thoughts faded from his mind, and he became clear and present in the moment.

Norman entered the room and walked to the closet. Jimmie saw his massive form through the slats of the door. Saw him reach for the handle. Heard the door shudder as he slid it open. That's when

Jimmie sprang on him. Threw himself against his massive frame, but he didn't budge, so Jimmie shoved his Smith and Wesson under the man's chin and squeezed the trigger.

The shot blew off the top of his bloated head and painted the ceiling red. He collapsed onto the floor. A large chunk of brain fell from his ruined skull, and blood soaked the beige carpet.

***

Jimmie's body tensed, and a blast of static shocked him from his trance. He'd forgotten that one. There were more repressed memories, and if he couldn't accept them he'd end up like James Bettencourt and all the others who'd killed themselves. Still, Jimmie didn't know what caused the sudden onslaught of guilt throughout the Louisville area, who was behind it, or why the effects were limited to Louisville? Was it some sort of broadcast? Subliminal? A signal with limited range? If so, what was the source? And who was behind it? The well-scrubbed man with the baton had said something about a reverend. Soon after that, he'd been repulsed by Peaches. What did all this have to do with the corpse? James Bettencourt's suicide note said he knew the fanatics would use it to kill "wayward souls." But how?

His mind swam with questions, as he stood and brushed dust from his clothes. Jimmie didn't know how close he was to breaking this case wide open. First, though, things would get a bit weird.

Pulling into the neon-lit parking lot of the Fog Light, Jimmie thought of Peaches. A blast of static hit him, as he tried to repress the memory of crushing her tender heart. He took a deep breath, exhaled with a huff, and let surface the memory of her on his cold linoleum floor. He'd been such an ass to judge her passionate behavior. Tears of regret trickled over his eyelids, and he bit his lip. That's when he saw Elaine Bettencourt's black Mercedes parked behind his office.

Jimmie pulled alongside her car and parked. Looking to his left, he saw she wasn't in the car. She was waiting inside for him, he supposed. Desire for her stirred through his body, and the static grew to the sound of bacon frying in a skillet. He took a deep breath and let it out gently. He'd accept whatever arose. Lust. Fear. Anger. Whatever.

Jimmie looked into the rearview. His eyes were tired. It had been a long day. The drive to Hamilton, Ohio. The strange occurrence at the red K sculpture, where a man disappeared before his eyes. Real life magic. Then the static and the memories. His recollection of blasting a man's skull to pieces. He was tired and unsure if he was ready to face what Elaine Bettencourt had in store. Had Mr. Magic found him worthy? Was she some sort of magician as well? Jimmie was in deep but had no idea what he was into. He stood for a moment to feel the fear in his body. The static settled to a low hiss, and he pushed open the door.

Looking into the back room, Jimmie saw the dark outline of his couch. A black rectangle on the grey floor. As he stood, his eyes adjusted so that he gradually made out the form of the widow sitting on his couch.

"Hello, Jimmie." Her voice slid through the darkness, echoed round the hollow space. Jimmie exhaled deeply, and let his body relax. Before he could ask what she was doing in his place, she cut him off. "We have to talk."

"Guess I'm worthy."

She chuckled at his insolence. "You are more than worthy. You will be a hero."

"I am a hero." He stepped into the room. "Haven't you heard?"

"Not like this. You could save countless lives, Jimmie. Keep this city from falling into the hands of religious extremists, idiots, and fools."

Pushing the door closed, Jimmie shut out the yellow and purple light from the club and peered into the darkness. There was still a bit of light coming through the large plate glass on the front of his office. Just enough for him to make his way to the couch and sit next to her.

"What did you think of 'Abracadabra'?"

"I think it's a funny word."

"Yeah."

"What does it have to do with me?"

"Everything, Jimmie." She shifted on the couch, "It has everything to do with you." She reached over to stroke his cheek, "Silly boy."

Jimmie leaned into her dark form and their lips met softly, deliciously. Warmth and delight travelled through his cheeks, and he surrendered to her. All resistance and fear drained from him, and they kissed. That's when the door swung open, and he saw the thin silhouette of Peaches.

Static hit hard, and he froze. All he could do was watch Peaches and Elaine stare at each other. It was a standoff between the woman who loved him and the mysterious interloper, Elaine Bettencourt. Who was she? What did she want? The detective didn't know but began to form an opinion when she raised her hand in the direction of Peaches and whisked her away with a dismissive gesture. Peaches turned and ran.

Next morning, Jimmie awoke with only sketchy memories of what she'd done or they'd done or whatever. All he knew was that he felt drained and depleted. So he headed to her place for a confrontation. When he got there, she met him at the door. Opened it before the detective even knocked.

"Hello, Jimmie."

"Hello my ass." He barged into the foyer and turned to face her. "What did you do to me?"

"What do you mean?" She looked baffled. "I did something to you?"

"Yes." He pressed his lips together and took a breath. "Last night."

"You don't remember?"

"Remember what?"

"We made love, and you gave me what I needed to reach the Reverend."

Jimmie shook his head. "What?" Confusion and disbelief swirled through his mind. "The Reverend? How do you know about him?"

"He's the one, Jimmie." She smiled kindly. "He's the one that had you beat. He has the corpse, and he's using it to power the broadcast. You know, the static." She took him by the hand, and started leading him upstairs. "He's trying to kill us all, Jimmie, with his guilt ray."

He couldn't believe his ears. She actually believed what she was saying, so he played along. "Where is this guilt ray? Perhaps we can destroy it."

"I don't know, but I know how to overcome its effects."

"How's that?"

"Come with me, and I'll show you."

Following her up the stairs, Jimmie recalled Peaches standing in his doorway. The static came over him like a tsunami, and his body grew tense. He stopped and stood still on a step. Elaine felt his reluctance and gave his hand a gentle tug. "Let's go, Jimmie. We must stop him before it's too late."

"How do we do that?"

"Follow me."

She led him to the right into her bedroom, where she turned to face him. "I want you to make love to me, Jimmie." She smiled. "I want you to do everything you want to do. Whatever you desire." She looked at him, ran a hand along his jaw. "Do you want that, Jimmie? Do you want rub my ass? Do you want to kiss my nipples? Do you want to fuck me? Whatever you want. You can have it."

"I don't understand. You bring me here, tell me to have my way, but what's in it for you?"

"What's in it for *us*, Jimmie, is that I will focus our energy into an attack against the Reverend. He killed my husband with that infernal signal, and I will use the energy we generate to form a psychic attack against him."

"What?"

She drew close to him, took his head and pressed his face into her long black hair. He smelled its vanilla scent, and the hissing static faded as he entered into the moment and accepted his longing for her.

"Hush, now." She whispered as she rubbed her cheek slowly on his bearded jaw and pressed herself against him. He felt her breasts compress against his chest and slipped an arm around her waist to pull her closer. Feeling her moist breath on his neck, he surrendered to the thrills that radiated through his body. His arousal intensified until all he wanted was the supreme joy of sexual union and release.

Jimmie wanted to stand back and watch her undress, so he broke free from her embrace and asked her to do it slowly. She smiled, happy to see he had joined the spirit of the proceedings.

She raised the black dress up to reveal her long legs. Their fine curves shone lustrously in black satin hose. She pulled the dress higher, and Jimmie saw the width of her hips and narrowness of her waist. She pulled it over her head and stood before him in a red and gold corset which barely contained her full breasts. His excitement grew, as he looked upon her hourglass figure and beautiful face. How many times had he imagined a woman like her? How many times had he made love to her in his dreams? She was perfection in flesh, and he wanted her more than he'd ever wanted anyone before.

She stood unflinching before him for a moment, gazed at him with her icy-blue eyes, then he slipped off his sports coat. Her eyes cut to the pistol in its shoulder holster.

"You don't need that thing." She whispered. "Get rid of it."

Jimmie removed the holster and put it on a nearby dresser. She came to him and began unbuttoning his shirt. He pushed his face again into her silky hair to inhale her intoxicating scent. It took but a moment for her to strip the shirt from him, and they pressed together with the mad exuberance of flesh on flesh. She led him toward the bed, where they fell with gasps and moans. Then, as a powerful rush of pleasure ran through his body, she writhed in ecstasy beneath him. Just as her pleasure built to a great climax, Jimmie sensed Elaine withdraw her consciousness and drift away as though she were in some other realm.

16a

When Jimmie woke, she came to him and asked if he remembered what they had done. He said he did.

"Good. You mustn't be ashamed, Jimmie." She sat on the edge of the bed beside him. "That's how it works, his guilt ray. It plays on your hang ups, regrets, and shame. It amplifies them to the point of paralyzing you with guilt. Every thought and desire is natural. It is a part of you, Jimmie. Some are dangerous or destructive. Gotta be careful with those. Let them flow by. Others are positive and life-affirming. Sexual desire, for example. There's lots of energy and power there. Resist it and you'll become a neurotic mess crippled by self-hate. Indulge it properly and your life force will grow. That's what we've been doing, Jimmie, sex magic."

"Well, I'm not as hung up as most folks. Sexually. But I do feel bad about Peaches. She really loves me. Wants the best for me. And you dismissed her so coldly. I did too."

The static started low and steady.

"What did you do, Jimmie?" She stroked his hair.

"I fucked her then threw her out." Static hissed through his tensing body, and he struggled to finish. Had to summon the courage to overcome his shame. "I called her a whore." Tears came to his eyes. They flowed down his face, and the static faded to a low hiss. His body relaxed and the tears flowed from deep within his soul. Tears of regret for Francesca and Mary and Peaches and infinite others.

"There, Jimmie, feel that energy. Feel the power of recovered memories. Use it. Focus your mind. Think about the corpse. I know you've seen it. Imagine the corpse. Tell me where it is."

He closed his eyes and brought up an image of the corpse. Lean body covered with leathery skin. Big bulging eyes. Lips parted to reveal white teeth, but one is missing.

The image began to rotate in his mind. It spun around and around, and he entered the vortex, until he was transported back in time. 1800's. More than that. Jimmie became the person, the living person, whose body presently was the mysterious mummy.

***

He was ill. Feverish and aching. Lying on his deathbed. The room spun around him. Slowly, it wobbled and spun. Just as the thought of unburdening his soul wobbled and spun through his mind.

"I must tell Finis Bates. He will believe my story. I can set the record straight. Reveal the whole plot. The long horseback ride to the checkpoint at Washington City. The meeting with Vice President Johnson. The dark theatre and a playbill advertising *Our American Cousin*. I'll tell him how I crept along a dark corridor, opened a door to see a small group, sitting on a balcony, then looked into my hand to see a derringer pistol. 'Sic semper tyrannis.' The phrase flowed through my mind. Deep. Resonant. Loud and proud. 'Sic semper tyrannis.' I will tell him my true name. I am John Wilkes Booth, and I am the assassin of President Lincoln."

***

Jimmie struggled to wake from the trance. Elaine had been on to something with all her talk of the liberation of repressed energy and psychic warfare and sex magic. They needed to compare notes and share their findings.

He rubbed a hand across his eyes. "Seems the corpse is John Wilkes Booth."

"The assassin?"

He nodded.

"That's interesting. Guess James got it while he was in New Orleans. Maybe a voodoo practitioner had it." She tilted her head.

"I think there was a plot with the Vice President." Jimmie shrugged. "A cover up." He took a deep breath and let it out quickly. "The mummy's in an underground bunker. That's the best I can do."

She raised her brows and tilted her head. "The Reverend is power mad and full of rage. A ranting fool, bent on the destruction of all who resist his feeble teachings."

"Is he a magician?" He scanned her face. "Like you?"

"Not like me." She shook her head. "I use natural, human emotions. Channel them to achieve peaceful aims." She smiled. "This guy wants to rule the world." Her face showed concern. "He's mad. Uses black magic. Dangerous stuff."

"And he has the corpse of John Wilkes Booth. What is he doing with it?"

"He's using it to power his guilt ray. He's using it to destroy his enemies."

"We've got to find it." I looked into her eyes. "Destroy it."

"Where do we start?"
"Google."

17a

Back in his office, Jimmie typed in "Louisville underground" and came up with the Mega Cavern. The website showed the Louisville skyline atop a huge hollow space and indicated 17 miles of tunnels that ran a hundred or so feet beneath the city. This looked like a good place to search for the mummy.

Reading further on the website, he learned the Mega Cavern featured, among other attractions, zip lines, guided tours, and bike courses. That was his best bet. He'd rent a bike and slip off the track to investigate.

***

Jimmie pedaled away from the rental office and into the dauntingly vast cavern. Managing to ride the easy trails, which offered plenty of opportunity to explore dark areas at the edges of the cavern. He looked for a side passage or door or anything that gave him goosebumps. Pretty soon Jimmie found an unmarked steel door secured with a chain and padlock. Looking over his shoulder, he leaned the bike against the limestone wall and set to work with his lock picking tools. Applying gentle pressure to the lock barrel and raking the tumblers with the pick, he popped the lock. Then he pulled the heavy chain from the steel handle, and slipped into the unlit passage.

He'd brought a flashlight to illuminate his further descent through the narrow limestone passage, and for the next two hours he walked to the rhythm of his scuffing shoes and watched the dimming circle of light skitter through the blackness. Jimmie was getting tired when he heard the echoing shouts and the gunfight between Mr. Eddie and Floyd.

***

Floyd James Hall was a teenage bellhop with dark brown hair, bright blue eyes, and a passion for reading Jimmie Star comics in the back of the daily paper. He followed the continuing adventures of Jimmie Star, private detective like other boys followed baseball and could recite every detail of the Jimmie's heroic struggles with Al Capone and other gangsters of the day. He'd cut each strip from the daily paper and paste them into a journal to form a single narrative, which he called *The Life and Times of Jimmie Star, Private Detective,* This book he kept in the pocket of his double-breasted bellhop's jacket and pulled out from time to time to review Jimmie's latest gun battle or fist fight.

The night had been slow at the Seelbach Hotel. There had been few arrivals and fewer departures, so Jimmie had had time to reread the latest episodes in which Jimmie Star faced down a bully and won the heart of the beautiful Lois. He was slipping the journal into his jacket pocket when he saw Mr. Eddie enter the hotel lobby.

Mr. Eddie was a regular at the hotel and a Chicago Outfit mobster, whose rackets included bootlegging, pornography, and prostitution. A large, stern man, Mr. Eddie wore a black suit with white pinstripes and a crimped white fedora. He held a girl of about eighteen close to his side.

"Evening, Mr. Eddie." Floyd's voice cracked, as fear tightened his vocal cords. "Checking in?"

The young woman's almond shaped face was framed by shiny blond hair cut in the bobbed style and topped with a soft cloche of the type worn by so many young women of the day.

"Yes." He smiled falsely. "Me and my daughter, Marie."

Sure thought Floyd. *Like your other daughters, she'll end up in a speakeasy brothel where anyone with a few bits can wallow between her legs till his heart's content.* "Right this way."

Floyd led the couple past the grand staircase to the arcing front desk and waited while Mr. Eddie checked in with the clerk. With Mr. Eddie distracted, Floyd looked at the girl, watched her squirm in Mr. Eddie's embrace. When He glanced at her face, Floyd noted the smooth roundness of her cheeks, the fearful set of her eyebrows, and the way her eyelashes clung together where tears had flowed.

Looking past Mr. Eddie's shoulder, she gazed toward Floyd, and when their eyes met he felt her fear.

"Your usual room: 217. Floyd will show you the way." The desk clerk smiled. "Hope you enjoy your stay."

Oh, yes, Mr. Eddie will enjoy his stay. He will enjoy his girl too. Use her up and throw her to the horny masses. A wave of anger passed through Floyd, who wished he had the courage to punch Mr. Eddie square in the jaw, *if I was Jimmie Star, I'd knock him into the thirties, leave only his white fedora, spinning and flipping slowly toward the marble floor.* His face flushed with a coward's shame when he gestured with an open hand for the couple to board the elevator.

"Second floor." Floyd was surprised by the flatness of his voice and manner in addressing the elevator operator. "Please."

As the elevator began to move, Floyd's body tensed. His arms trembled with the desire to blast a hole in Mr. Eddie's skull. He burned with the longing to splatter his blood and brains across every surface of the elevator car just as he imagined Jimmie Star would do.

The operator slid open the elevator doors. Floyd managed a tight-lipped smile, while he waited for Mr. Eddie and Claire to cross the threshold.

At the door to room 217, Mr. Eddie pulled a brown envelope from his jacket pocket.

"You might like these." He pressed the envelope into Floyd's hand.

Floyd watched Mr. Eddie, holding the girl firmly, enter the room and close the door.

Worry filled Floyd's heart, as he slid the envelope into his jacket pocket and walked dejectedly to the back stairs and descended to the basement, where he entered the locker room. He opened the envelope and pulled out a small stack of black and white photographs of girls and women, mostly nude, mostly bound and unhappy. As he looked through the stack, Floyd recognized one of the girls. It was Mr. Eddie's companion.

Floyd's heart fluttered as he looked at the image. The young flapper, who a moment before had been within reach, stood with her hands bound above her head, loose dress hitched over her hips to reveal her round bottom. A scowling man with a pair of rimless round glasses held a bundle of switches, about to spank her tender rear. She looked back across her shoulder, an expression of trepidation on her face.

Floyd wanted to hold her in his arms and stroke her worried brow until the fear retreated from her eyes, and she shone like the morning sun. He put the envelope back into his jacket and returned to his post, but the image of the girl's worried expression stayed with him. It called to his conscience as the evening dragged out and concern overwhelmed his workman's diligence. That's when Floyd decided to investigate.

Looking over his shoulder, he slipped away from the lobby and made his way to the back stairs. Once inside the stairwell, he glanced toward the basement and subbasement, then began to climb.

At the second floor, he opened the door to the hallway, and looked down the corridor to see it empty. He walked down the passage and slowed as he approached room 217. He looked again down the hall then pressed his ear to the door to hear the deep voice of Mr. Eddie.

Glancing over his shoulder, Floyd dropped to a knee, leaned toward the door, and peered through the keyhole. By the yellowish light of the bedside lamp, he saw the girl: kneeling, wearing only a robe and a leather collar around her neck. Standing before her, Mr. Eddie held the leash.

"Almost time for the offering, my virgin girl." Mr. Eddie looked down on her. "Oh, It will love you." He stroked her tear-streaked cheek. "Your lovely curves will make him quiver with delight. And your succulent flesh. So sweet to touch. It's an honor, really." He smiled briefly. "Time to go."

"I can't."

"Get up." Mr. Eddie tugged the leash.

"I can't"

"I said 'get up.'"

He dragged her across the carpet to the nightstand to pick up a knife.

Floyd's heart sputtered when he saw light glint from the blade, and he accidentally rattled the doorknob.

The young woman shifted her gaze and strained her eyes in an effort to stare through the keyhole. Fearing that the person on the other side of the door would be the last person to see her alive and hoping that it was the handsome and caring bellhop, the girl called out, "I'm Claire!"

Mr. Eddie yanked the leash, and her body skittered across the carpet.

Floyd's heart stuttered. Fierce energy coursed through his body, tears streamed down his cheeks, and he saw the image of his Colt 1911 pistol sitting in his locker downstairs. *I will kill the bastard.*

Floyd ran down the hall to the stairwell and descended to the basement. Bloody images flashed through his mind. Splattering blood and shards of bone. Bits of brain on the wall. Mr. Eddie collapsing in a red mist.

Floyd entered the locker room, pulled the keys from his pocket, and struggled with quivering hands to open the lock. He threw open the door and reached inside to find his pistol.

With fury in his eyes, Floyd swung open the stairwell door. Stepping through the opening, he heard Claire whimper and the door to the subbasement close. For a moment, he stood motionless, grinding his teeth and squinting his eyes.

Floyd crept down the steps, until he reached the door to the subbasement. Taking the cold brass handle in his hand, he slowly ease the door open. He stepped into the poorly-lit, cave-like chamber beneath the foundations of the grand hotel, eased the heavy door into its frame, and then turned to look into the murky space.

As his eyes adjusted to the darkness, he heard the reverberating sounds of water dripping, the scuffing of feet, and his own panting. Then he saw, in the near distance, Mr. Eddie, leading Claire through the stony rubble.

Floyd kneaded the handle of the pistol in his sweaty hand, drew a hissing breath, and rose to follow the sounds and half glimpses of movement until Mr. Eddie stopped on a stone platform at the edge of a large pool of black water. Floyd ducked behind a boulder to observe. That's when he heard the jangle and scuff of heavy chains.

After removing the girl's robe, Mr. Eddie bound her wrists with handcuffs connected to long chains, which extended to supporting columns. He stood before her and held the blade to her cheek.

In darkness, Floyd raised the Colt and tried to aim it at Mr. Eddie, but his hand shook violently. He tried to pull the trigger but couldn't. Every effort to squeeze the trigger produced more quivering instead. Tears of frustration filled his eyes. He blinked hard, lowered the 1911, and watched Mr. Eddie slice through the tender flesh of Claire's cheek. He watched her blood flow from the shallow wound down her chin onto her breasts. Mr. Eddie took a handkerchief from his pocket, shook it open, and rubbed her chest lustily until the white cloth was stained red with her blood.

"It will be pleased." Mr. Eddie turned away from her and walked a couple steps to the pool. He held the handkerchief above the dark water and squeezed Claire's blood from it. The blood dissolved into the water and dispersed throughout the underground lake to attract It to the sacrifice.

Exhausted from her ordeal, Claire hung loosely from the cuffs. Blood flowed down her stomach to her leg and across her foot to the flat stone then continued in crooked rivulets toward the black water.

Following the blood trail, It set off through the dark water with an entrancing light show from its many tentacles which swayed and curled behind the bulk of its massive body. It shimmied through the featureless depth where it had existed and held sway over the hearts of men since the founding of the city of Louisville. Rising now through a dim shaft of light, It neared the surface but turned back just beneath the surface causing the water to swirl and splash against the irregular edges of the pool.

Mr. Eddie stared at the roiling water, watched the surface shimmer in the dim light of his fading flashlight. The movement intensified until the undulating water began to splash over the edges of the stone platform, and Mr. Eddie, giddy with delight, laughed like an infant gone silly over a game of peekaboo. Then something broke the surface of the water.

A tentacle rose from the water to curl and writhe high above Claire. It was mottled purple and green, thick as a mature oak tree at the surface of the water, and tapered down to a point at the end of its thirty foot swaying length. It undulated toward Claire, who slumped stuporously in the cuffs. It licked its goo-coated tentacle across her bloody cheek, then entered her open mouth and slid across her tongue. Meanwhile another massive tentacle rose from the water to grope her leg.

Claire bit down hard on the tough tentacle and broke its leathery skin. Her mouth filled with a spurt of gelatinous goo, which flowed across her lips and

275

dripped from her chin. The tentacle jerked back, and the other yanked her feet from beneath her. The chains went taut with a clank, and her hands began to slip through the handcuffs, shedding skin as they scraped against the cold, grey metal.

Her head tossed back, as her body, suspended between the chains and the tentacle, writhed in the thing's grasp. High above, the injured tentacle swung and whipped with increasing speed.

"Please!" Claire screamed. "Someone help!"

Feeling the pistol shake in his hand, Floyd took a quivering breath and stepped from the darkness. He raised the pistol, aimed it at the strange thing, and squeezed the trigger. The flash of fire from the muzzle shocked him, and the shot missed. As the echoing boom faded, Floyd approached Claire. He aimed the Colt again at the thick base of the tentacle. He fired and hit the tentacle wrapped around her leg. It jerked spastically and sprayed goo. Floyd fired again. More goo splashed from the thing, and it released Claire to whip through the air in a wild, serpentine display of frustration and fury.

Aiming the gun steadily, Floyd squeezed the trigger smoothly. The shot passed through both tentacles, which then twisted together and withdrew beneath the surface of the black water. Then Floyd turned toward Mr. Eddie, hiding behind a boulder. He saw the blast from Mr. Eddie's revolver and felt the bullet bore through his shoulder. His body jerked back, but fury drove him toward the boulder and Mr. Eddie.

As Floyd approached, Mr. Eddie rose. The two men, guns held level, faced each other.

Mr. Eddie studied Floyd, noticed the fierceness of his expression, and knew the spirit of Jimmie Star had risen in his soul. He dug in his pocket and pulled out his keys.

"Have her." Mr. Eddie tossed the keys to Floyd. "She's yours."

Rage swelled in Floyd, and steely determination drove him toward justice. His finger pressed against the trigger just as Mr. Eddie clinched his. The simultaneous gunfire filled the subbasement with a tremendous, reverberating boom, and Mr. Eddie fell back, clutching his stomach.

Floyd walked toward the fallen man, who fired wildly, until the hammer of his pistol fell with a dry click on a spent cartridge. Then Floyd looked down to see Mr. Eddie's grimacing.

"Now." Floyd commanded. "Get in the water."

"Wha-- What?" Sweat dripped from Mr. Eddie's face.

"Into the water." Floyd pointed the gun at his head. "It's an honor, really." He jabbed Mr. Eddie with the pistol.

Floyd grabbed Mr. Eddie by the hair and pulled him up to his knees. "Get going." He tugged Mr. Eddie, who crawled reluctantly across the jagged stone rubble to the edge of the pool, where he gazed at the black water to see his own face reflected. A tentacle ripped through the surface of the water to wrap the gangster in a suffocating, bone-crushing embrace and drag him into the limitless depth.

Using Mr. Eddie's keys, Floyd freed Claire from the shackles, wrapped her in his jacket, and gazed deeply into her tired eyes hoping to see the spark of eternal love.

***

That's when Jimmie burst in looking down the barrel of his Smith and Wesson to see a bellhop holding a nearly naked girl. The girl's face and wrists were bleeding, and the bellhop held a pistol.

Jimmie's eyes met Floyd's, and they smiled with recognition. Floyd was a projection from Jimmie's mind into the past. One of his poorly-managed bodhisattva powers. He could emanate splinters of himself to the various realms and times. Now and then these splinters return to him bringing the experiences they'd had, so it was no great surprise to Jimmie when the space between them began to glow with the flow of energy from Floyd.

Nor did Floyd seem to mind the diminishment of his being. To the contrary, he appeared to relish the tingling in his body and the rush of memories through his mind as his form gradually dissolved like a television image fading out pixel by pixel. The image faded to static then disappeared into Jimmie, as he absorbed the last bit of energy and data from Floyd and put an end to his phantasmal existence.

Clare, shivering with awe and wonder, curled into a tight ball when Jimmie approached her and bent down to collect Floyd's Colt 1911.

"Come now darling." He smiled "Let's take you home."

"Don't have a home."

"No parents? Family?"

She shook her head.

"Then come with me. I'll protect you."

"Where will we go?"

"The future. 2018." He shrugged. "I hope."

18a

After retrieving Claire's clothes and shoes from the room, Jimmie returned to the subbasement to find her hiding in a corner behind a wooden crate marked: DUPONT EXPLOSIVE. Those markings caught his attention, so, while Clare dressed, he set to work opening the crate. When he couldn't open it with his bare hands, Jimmie grabbed a large stone and smashed the corner until straw stuffing began to fall out. Then the detective kneeled next to the crate and stuck a hand into it. After pulling out more moldy straw, he found what he'd expected and hoped to find.

Dynamite and blasting caps and wire left over from the recent construction had been stored and forgotten in a corner of the subbasement. Never one to let an opportunity pass, Jimmie carefully gathered two sticks, two caps, and a spool of wire then set off with Claire down the narrow tunnel toward the Mega Cavern and 15 March 2018.

Along the way Claire told her story. It went like this:

"I was a Catholic school girl. My family lived in Oak Park just outside of downtown Chicago, and my parents were strict true believers: guilt-stricken and ashamed, and they kept me on the straight and narrow until they died in an automobile accident. After that, I kinda lost my way. Just a little. I started hanging out in the speakeasies. Listening to jazz and drinking illicit liquor. Things never got outta hand until Mr. Eddie started talking to me about how pure and innocent I was. Then he asked if I wanted to take a ride in his '26 Cadillac Town Sedan. Well, I jumped at the chance and ended up chained to a pillar in the subbasement of that hotel. Then this thing came up from an underground lake.

It was all tentacles and slime. It tried to take me under, but Floyd saved me. He killed Mr. Eddie too. That's when you came in and absorbed him or whatever."

About that time, Jimmie noticed something he'd missed on the first trip through the passage. A small opening at the bottom of the wall. Just a slit barely large enough for him to shimmy through. When Jimmie knelt beside it, he heard a low drone, which piqued his interest, so he got on his stomach and worked through the tight passage, which thankfully opened into a smooth, concrete tunnel about eight feet high. Jimmie called to Claire to follow, but she hesitated.

"I'm scared."

"You can do it."

"But why should I?"

"We must destroy the corpse of John Wilke Booth."

"Mister, you're zozzled."

"Am I?" He paused. "You saw what happened to Floyd. You saw what came outta that lake. There's some wild stuff goin' on, and people are losing their lives because of that damn mummy. I don't think I can do it alone. I need your help."

No response.

"Please."

That's when she came through to join him in the tunnel, where the hum sounded like electricity zapping through a wire. The detective had to investigate the source, so they started along the inclining tunnel toward the noise, but they didn't make it far before he began to suffer recollections of Michael Murphy.

It started with his fist crossing Michael's jaw and the good feeling that brought. The elation of smashing that traitor to love right in the face gave way to an image of the rough brown rope around Michael's wrists. Then the static hit. It zapped Jimmie hard, tensed his neck and jaws, and sent a spasm through his body, which made him drop Mr. Eddie's flashlight. Luckily it still worked when, after letting pass the bothersome memories, Jimmie picked it up and tested it.

They continued up the tunnel, but when he recalled the slice he'd made in Michael Murphy's gut and felt the flow of warm blood across his hand, Jimmie was struck by such a strong blast of static that his whole body locked up in a grand mal seizure, and he fell to the concrete floor.

Claire came to him and stroked his cheek.

"Are you okay?

It took a while for him to reply. "It's here. The mummy."

"What?"

"Listen. You gotta do as I ask." Jimmie looked into her eyes. "It'll save the city from oppression."

"What do you want him to do?"

"I can't go on. The pain is too much. I need you to find it. Find it and destroy it. Take this dynamite. When you find the corpse put these under it, attach the wire, and run it back to me." He handed her the explosive sticks with primers attached and the spool of wire.

She looked at him quizzically.

"Please," Jimmie stared into her eyes, "you are pure of heart and unaffected by the guilt ray. Only you can do it."

She nodded and turned to go just as he recalled reaching his hand through the slit in Michael Murphy's gut to pull out a thick strand of innards. A crippling shock of static curled him into the fetal position, but Jimmie managed to gasp, "Hurry."

Claire ran up the incline to a corner in the tunnel and went around it to the right. When she did she saw natural light in the distance. She was just beneath the surface, and heard automobile traffic noises mix with the electronic hum. Continuing beneath and beyond the overhead opening, she soon found a door to the right.

Jimmie was able to accept the memory of pulling Michael Murphy's guts from his stomach while Murphy trembled before him. They were on the Big Four Bridge, and he was tying the loose end to a girder. The night was still and cold, and his breath fogged from his mouth. "Onto the rail. Get on the rail and dance."

Static hit hard, and Jimmie struggled to breathe, as sweat poured from his face.

Passing through the doorway, Claire saw the mummified corpse of John Wilkes Booth on a concrete platform. There were wires coming out from various body parts. They travelled to a bank of electronics with several small red and green lights that blinked. From there a single, thick wire went up into the concrete ceiling.

Claire walked to the corpse and reached out a delicate white hand to take hold of the arm, covered with dark, leathery skin. She tilted the body away from her slightly and slid the sticks of dynamite beneath it. She left the blasting caps exposed so she could attach the wire. When she had done so, she retreated toward the detective, lying on the concrete floor.

By this time he'd managed to accept the memory of Michael Murphy dancing nude on the rail of the Big Four Bridge. The glistening strap of his intestines stretched from the slit in his stomach to the girder that he'd tied it to. Drawing a deep breath, Jimmie struggled to relax. As he let the breath pass, he recalled Michael's nervous jittering beneath the sliver moon and the chill from the river running below. He saw the puff of his breath when he said, "Jump."

"Wha-"

"Jump."

When Michael looked over the edge of the bridge and saw the pale moonlight shimmering on the Ohio River below, Jimmie shook his head, and he saw the tears trickle down his ashen face and felt a slight twinge of doubt. Was this the way of a Bodhisattva? Was this the hand of a future Buddha pushing a man to his death?

Michael disappeared over the railing. He descended toward the river, as his guts played out behind him then went taut.

The body of Michael Murphy swayed, slow and silent, high above the river.

When Claire turned the corner and saw him crying on the cold concrete, she called out, "Jimmie," and hurried toward him.

"You found it?"

"Yes."

"Okay. Let's blow it up."

Claire handed him the spool with the little remaining wire. He pulled it loose and took Mr. Eddie's flashlight from his pocket.

"Get on the floor behind me. Be ready."

Jimmie removed the battery and, looked across his shoulder to see Claire curled up in a tight ball, and then he touched the end of the wire to the battery.

The explosion filled the room with an orange fireball that expanded down the tunnel and around the corner toward them. Luckily it faded out before reaching them. There was a tremendous rumbling of rubble, as the transmission room collapsed, and a dark cloud of dust engulfed them.

After the dust settled, they made their way into the Louisville Mega Cavern and out to the parking lot. Jimmie worried that the time wasn't right but felt better when he saw his Beemer waiting there. When they got in, he turned on the radio and heard the local news.

"Officials on the scene of today's explosion at the University of Louisville have still not determined the cause. It appears to have been centered in the service tunnels that run beneath the campus. Police and Fire officials speculate there may have been a gas leak. One thing is certain: the foundations of the Confederate Soldier's Memorial Monument has been badly damaged. The seventy foot tall structure is leaning badly toward the North and will most likely need to be removed."

Jimmie put two and two together when he heard that the reliquary chamber was beneath the Confederate Monument. That's when he knew the reverend was using the tower to transmit his guilt signal. Everything made sense.

When Jimmie pulled the BMW onto the onramp to the Waterson Expressway and punched the gas, Claire was amazed by the car's speed. As he headed East on the freeway, she marveled at the variety of automobiles and their bright colors. But by the time he'd pulled off the road in front of Elaine Bettencourt's, Claire was beginning to tire out from her time travelling adventure. She would need help recovering and adjusting, and he had a plan.

When Elaine opened the door and saw them, she threw her arms around him and said, "I don't know how you did it, but you did. You saved the city."

"It's all in a day's work. Meet Claire. She's the true hero."

"Come in. Sit. Tell me everything."

"I really can't. Gotta see somebody. But Claire could use a place to stay and a friend."

"She has both right here." Elaine patted Claire's shoulder. "Are you going after the Reverend?"

"No. He's harmless now."

Jimmie turned toward the door, but Elaine stopped him with a hug.

"Bless you, Jimmie Star."

19a

Back in his office on Berry Boulevard, Jimmie wanted to crash on the old leather couch. He needed to, but there was still the problem of Peaches. He'd hurt her and needed to make things right, so he walked next door to the Fog Light Club. Passing through the door, he felt the rush of memories. Peaches lying on his floor. Candy lying across his bed. The murders. He'd have eternity to pay for his deeds, but he'd start right then.

Peaches saw him standing just inside the door, and tears rushed to her eyes. She broke a little, and he went through the purple and yellow and chrome of the Fog Light to hold her in his arms. Jimmie made no excuses. He told no stories but simply held her close as her tears soaked through his shirt and his flowed down his nose into her hair.

"I'm sorry," he said.

At that moment, Sal Luca, Doc Laraunt's former associate, stepped from a booth in the darkness of the Fog Light Club. He took one large step toward Jimmie from behind. Extending his arm to place the muzzle of his Glock 9mm against the side of Jimmie's head, the gangster pulled the trigger.

Jimmie experienced an infinitesimal moment of pain followed by a blast of clear and pure consciousness by which he knew himself not as a person but as an unbound awareness and intention with infinite reach. He could travel the galaxies with the slightest wish and sit with the Buddhas of all epochs. But all too soon the energetic force of karma found him, and as he realized that he was being drawn back into the realm of suffering, Jimmie became frantic and called out to the Bodhisattva Avaloketeshvara, who appeared to him in the midst of a red light that gleamed around her. She recognized him as a fellow bodhisattva, tainted and misguided perhaps, and certainly driven by the storms of karma still, but willing and intending to end the suffering of all beings in all realms and "times." She radiated her blessing to him to ease his heart, as the momentum of his thoughts and deeds pushed him toward his next incarnation.